Flaxman Low, Occult Psychologist Collected Stories

By

E. and H. Heron

Cover Photograph: quapan

ISBN: 978-1-78139-325-3

Contents

The Story of the Spaniards, Hammersmith

HAVE ghosts any existence outside our own fancy and emotions? This is the question with which the end of the century concerns itself more and more, for, though a vast amount of evidence with regard to occult phenomena already exists, the ultimate answer has yet to be supplied. In this connection it may not generally be known that, as one of the first steps towards reducing Psychology to the lines of an exact science, an attempt has been made to classify spirits and ghosts, with the result that some very bizarre and terrible theories have been put forward--things undreamt of outside the circle of the select few.

With a view to meeting the widespread interest in these matters, the following series of ghost stories is laid before the public. They have been gathered out of a large number of supernatural experiences with which Mr. Flaxman Low--under the thin disguise of which name many are sure to recognise one of the leading scientists of the day, with whose works on Psychology and kindred subjects they are familiar-- has been more or less connected. He is, moreover, the first student in this field of inquiry who has had the boldness and originality to break free from old and conventional methods, and to approach the elucidation of so-called supernatural problems on the lines of natural law.

The details of these stories have been supplied by the narratives of those most concerned, supplemented by the clear and ample notes which Mr. Flaxman Low has had the courtesy to place in our hands.

For obvious reasons, the exact localities where these events are said to have happened are in every case merely indicated.

No. I.--THE STORY OF THE SPANIARDS, HAMMERSMITH.

LIEUTENANT RODERICK HOUSTON, of H.M.S. Sphinx, had practically nothing beyond his pay, and he was beginning to be very tired of the West African station, when he received the pleasant intelligence that a relative had left him a legacy. This consisted of a satisfactory sum in ready money and a house in Hammersmith, which was rated at over £200 a year, and was said in addition to be comfortably furnished. Houston, therefore, counted on its rental to bring his income up to a fairly desirable figure. Further information from home, however, showed him that he had been rather premature in his expectations, whereupon, being a man of action, he applied for two months' leave, and came home to look after his affairs himself.

When he had been a week in London he arrived at the conclusion that he could not possibly hope single-handed to tackle the difficulties which presented themselves. He accordingly wrote the following letter to his friend, Flaxman Low:

"The Spaniards, Hammersmith, 23-3-1892.

"DEAR LOW,--Since we parted some three years ago, I have heard very little of you. It was only yesterday that I met our mutual friend, Sammy Smith ('Silkworm' of our schooldays) who told me that your studies have developed in a new direction, and that you are now a good deal interested in psychical subjects. If this be so, I hope to induce you to come and stay with me here for a few days by promising to introduce you to a problem in your own line. I am just now living at 'The Spaniards,' a house that has lately been left to me, and which in the first instance was built by an old fellow named Van Nuysen, who married a great-aunt of mine. It is a good house, but there is said to be 'something wrong' with it. It lets easily, but unluckily the tenants cannot be persuaded to remain above a week or two. They complain that the place is haunted by something--presumably a ghost--because its vagaries bear just that brand of inconsequence which stamps the common run of manifestations.

"It occurs to me that you may care to investigate the matter with me. If so, send me a wire when to expect you.

"Yours ever.

"RODERICK HOUSTON."

Houston waited in some anxiety for an answer. Low was the sort of man one could rely on in almost any emergency. Sammy Smith had told him a characteristic anecdote of Low's career at Oxford, where, although his intellectual triumphs may be forgotten, he will always be remembered by the story that when Sands, of Queen's, fell ill on the day before the 'Varsity sports, a telegram was sent to Low's rooms: "Sands ill. You must do the hammer for us." Low's reply was pithy: "I'll be there." Thereupon he finished the treatise upon which he was engaged, and next day his strong, lean figure was to be seen swinging

2

the hammer amidst vociferous cheering, for that was the occasion on which he not only won the event, but beat the record.

On the fifth day Low's answer came from Vienna. As he read it, Houston recalled the high forehead, long neck--with its accompanying low collar--and thin moustache of his scholarly, athletic friend, and smiled. There was so much more in Flaxman Low than anyone gave him credit for.

"MY DEAR HOUSTON,--Very glad to hear of you again. In response to your kind invitation, I thank you for the opportunity of meeting the ghost, and still more for the pleasure of your companionship. I came here to inquire into a somewhat similar affair. I hope, however, to be able to leave to-morrow, and will be with you some time on Friday evening.

"Very sincerely yours.

"FLAXMAN LOW."

"P.S.--By the way, will it be convenient to give your servants a holiday during the term of my visit, as, if my investigations are to be of any value, not a grain of dust must be disturbed in your house, excepting by ourselves?--F.L."

"The Spaniards" was within some fifteen minutes' walk of Hammersmith Bridge. Set in the midst of a fairly respectable neighbourhood, it presented an odd contrast to the commonplace dullness of the narrow streets crowded about it. As Flaxman Low drove up in the evening light, he reflected that the house might have come from the back of beyond--it gave an impression of something old-world and something exotic.

It was surrounded by a ten-foot wall, above which the upper storey was visible, and Low decided that this intensely English house still gave some curious suggestion of the tropics. The interior of the house carried out the same idea, with its sense of space and air, cool tints and wide, matted passages.

"So you have seen something yourself since you came?" Low said, as they sat at dinner, for Houston had arranged that meals should be sent in for them from an hotel.

"I've heard tapping up and down the passage upstairs. It is an uncarpeted landing which runs the whole length of the house. One night, when I was quicker than usual, I saw what looked like a bladder disappear into one of the bedrooms--your room it is to be, by the way--and the door closed behind it," replied Houston discontentedly. "The usual meaningless antics of a ghost."

"What had the tenants who lived here to say about it?" went on Low.

"Most of the people saw and heard just what I have told you, and promptly went away. The only one who stood out for a little while was old Filderg--you know the man? Twenty years ago he made an effort to cross the Australian deserts--he stopped for eight weeks. When he left he saw the house-agent, and said he was afraid he had done a little shooting practice in the upper passage, and he hoped it wouldn't count against him in the bill, as it was done in defence of his life. He said something had jumped on to the bed and tried to strangle him. He described it as cold and glutinous, and he pursued it down the passage, firing at it. He advised the owner to have the house pulled down; but, of course, my cousin did nothing of the kind. It's a very good house, and he did not see the sense of spoiling his property."

"That's very true," replied Flaxman Low, looking round. "Mr. Van Nuysen had been in the West Indies, and kept his liking for spacious rooms."

"Where did you hear anything about him?" asked Houston in surprise.

"I have heard nothing beyond what you told me in your letter; but I see a couple of bottles of Gulf weed and a lace-plant ornament, such as people used to bring from the West Indies in former days."

"Perhaps I should tell you the history of the old man," said Houston doubtfully; "but we aren't proud of it!"

Flaxman Low considered a moment.

"When was the ghost seen for the first time?"

"When the first tenant took the house. It was let after old Van Nuysen's time."

"Then it may clear the way if you will tell me something of him."

"He owned sugar plantations in Trinidad, where he passed the greater part of his life, while his wife mostly remained in England--incompatibility of temper it was said. When he came home for good and built this house they still lived apart, my aunt declaring that nothing on earth would persuade her to return to him. In course of time he became a confirmed invalid, and he then insisted on my aunt joining him. She lived here for perhaps a year, when she was found dead in bed one morning--in your room."

"What caused her death?"

"She had been in the habit of taking narcotics, and it was supposed that she smothered herself while under their influence."

"That doesn't sound very satisfactory," remarked Flaxman Low.

4

"Her husband was satisfied with it anyhow, and it was no one else's business. The family were only too glad to have the affair hushed up."

"And what became of Mr. Van Nuysen?"

"That I can't tell you. He disappeared a short time after. Search was made for him in the usual way, but nobody knows to this day what became of him."

"Ah, that was strange, as he was such an invalid," said Low, and straightway fell into a long fit of abstraction, from which he was roused by hearing Houston curse the incurable foolishness and imbecility of ghostly behaviour. Flaxman woke up at this. He broke a walnut thoughtfully and began in a gentle voice:

"My dear fellow, we are apt to be hasty in our condemnation of the general behaviour of ghosts. It may appear incalculably foolish in our eyes, and I admit there often seems to be a total absence of any apparent object or intelligent action. But remember that what appears to us to be foolishness may be wisdom in the spirit world, since our unready senses can only catch broken glimpses of what is, I have not the slightest doubt, a coherent whole, if we could trace the connection."

"There may be something in that," replied Houston indifferently. "People naturally say that this ghost is the ghost of old Van Nuysen. But what connection can possibly exist between what I have told you of him and the manifestations--a tapping up and down the passage and the drawing about of a bladder like a child at play? It sounds idiotic!"

"Certainly. Yet it need not necessarily be so. There are isolated facts, we must look for the links which lie between. Suppose a saddle and a horse-shoe were to be shown to a man who had never seen a horse, I doubt whether he, however intelligent, could evolve the connecting idea! The ways of spirits are strange to us simply because we need further data to help us to interpret them."

"It's a new point of view," returned Houston, "but upon my word, you know, Low, I think you're wasting your time!"

Flaxman Low smiled slowly; his grave, melancholy face brightened.

"I have," said he, "gone somewhat deeply into the subject. In other sciences one reasons by analogy. Psychology is unfortunately a science with a future but without a past, or more probably it is a lost science of the ancients. However that may be, we stand to-day on the frontier of an unknown world, and progress is the result of individual effort; each solution of difficult phenomena forms a step towards the solution of the next problem. In this case, for example, the bladder-like object may be the key to the mystery."

Houston yawned.

"It all seems pretty senseless, but perhaps you may be able to read reason into it. If it were anything tangible, anything a man could meet with his fists, it would be easier."

"I entirely agree with you. But suppose we deal with this affair as it stands, on similar lines, I mean on prosaic, rational lines, as we should deal with a purely human mystery."

"My dear fellow," returned Houston, pushing his chair back from the table wearily, "you shall do just as you like, only get rid of the ghost!"

For some time after Low's arrival nothing very special happened. The tappings continued, and more than once Low had been in time to see the bladder disappear into the closing door of his bedroom, though, unluckily, he never chanced to be inside the room on these occasions, and however quickly he followed the bladder, he never succeeded in seeing anything further. He made a thorough examination of the house, and left no space unaccounted for in his careful measurement. There were no cellars, and the foundation of the house consisted of a thick layer of concrete.

At length, on the sixth night, an event took place, which, as Flaxman Low remarked, came very near to putting an end to the investigations as far as he was concerned. For the preceding two nights he and Houston had kept watch in the hope of getting a glimpse of the person or thing which tapped so persistently up and down the passage. But they were disappointed, for there were no manifestations. On the third evening, therefore, Low went off to his room a little earlier than usual, and fell asleep almost immediately.

He says he was awakened by feeling a heavy weight upon his feet, something that seemed inert and motionless. He recollected that he had left the gas burning, but the room was now in darkness.

Next he was aware that the thing on the bed had slowly shifted, and was gradually travelling up towards his chest. How it came on the bed he had no idea. Had it leaped or climbed? The sensation he experienced as it moved was of some ponderous, pulpy body, not crawling or creeping, but spreading! It was horrible! He tried to move his lower limbs, but could not because of the deadening weight. A feeling of drowsiness began to overpower him, and a deadly cold, such as he said he had before felt at sea when in the neighbourhood of icebergs, chilled upon the air.

With a violent struggle he managed to free his arms, but the thing grew more irresistible as it spread upwards. Then he became conscious

6

of a pair of glassy eyes, with livid, everted lids, looking into his own. Whether they were human eyes or beast eyes, he could not tell, but they were watery, like the eyes of a dead fish, and gleamed with a pale, internal lustre.

Then he owns he grew afraid. But he was still cool enough to notice one peculiarity about this ghastly visitant--although the head was within a few inches of his own, he could detect no breathing. It dawned on him that he was about to be suffocated, for, by the same method of extension, the thing was now coming over his face! It felt cold and clammy, like a mass of mucilage or a monstrous snail. And every instant the weight became greater. He is a powerful man, and he struck with his fists again and again at the head. Some substance yielded under the blows with a sickening sensation of bruised flesh.

With a lucky twist he raised himself in the bed and battered away with all the force he was capable of in his cramped position. The only effect was an occasional shudder or quake that ran through the mass as his half-arm blows rained upon it. At last, by chance, his hand knocked against the candle beside him. In a moment he recollected the matches. He seized the box, and struck a light.

As he did so, the lump slid to the floor. He sprang out of bed, and lit the candle. He felt a cold touch upon his leg, but when he looked down there was nothing to be seen. The door, which he had locked overnight, was now open, and he rushed out into the passage. All was still and silent with the throbbing vacancy of night time.

After searching round, he returned to his room. The bed still gave ample proof of the struggle that had taken place, and by his watch he saw the hour to be between two and three.

As there seemed nothing more to be done, he put on his dressing-gown, lit his pipe, and sat down to write an account of the experience he had just passed through for the Psychical Research Society--from which paper the above is an abstract.

He is a man of strong nerves, but he could not disguise from himself that he had been at handgrips with some grotesque form of death. What might be the nature of his assailant he could not determine, but his experience was supported by the attack which had been made on Filderg, and also--it was impossible to avoid the conclusion--by the manner of Mrs. Van Nuysen's death.

He thought the whole situation over carefully in connection with the tapping and the disappearing bladder, but, turn these events how he would, he could make nothing of them. They were entirely incongruous. A little later he went and made a shakedown in Houston's room.

"What was the thing?" asked Houston, when Low had ended his story of the encounter.

Low shrugged his shoulders.

"At least it proves that Filderg did not dream," he said.

"But this is monstrous! We are more in the dark than ever. There's nothing for it but to have the house pulled down. Let us leave to-day."

"Don't be in a hurry, my dear fellow. You would rob me of a very great pleasure; besides, we may be on the verge of some valuable discovery. This series of manifestations is even more interesting than the Vienna mystery I was telling you of."

"Discovery or not," replied the other, "I don't like it."

The first thing next morning Low went out for a quarter of an hour. Before breakfast a man with a barrowful of sand came into the garden. Low looked up from his paper, leant out of the window, and gave some order.

When Houston came down a few minutes later he saw the yellowish heap on the lawn with some surprise.

"Hullo! What's this?" he asked.

"I ordered it," replied Low.

"All right. What's it for?"

"To help us in our investigations. Our visitor is capable of being felt, and he or it left a very distinct impression on the bed. Hence I gather it can also leave an impression on sand. It would be an immense advance if we could arrive at any correct notion of what sort of feet the ghost walks on. I propose to spread a layer of this sand in the upper passage, and the result should be footmarks if the tapping comes to-night."

That evening the two men made a fire in Houston's bedroom, and sat there smoking and talking, to leave the ghost "a free run for once," as Houston phrased it. The tapping was heard at the usual hour, and presently the accustomed pause at the other end of the passage and the quiet closing of the door.

Low heaved a long sigh of satisfaction as he listened.

"That's my bedroom door," he said; "I know the sound of it perfectly. In the morning, and with the help of daylight, we shall see what we shall see."

As soon as there was light enough for the purpose of examining the footprints, Low roused Houston.

Houston was full of excitement as a boy, but his spirits fell by the time he had passed from end to end of the passage.

"There are marks," he said, "but they are as perplexing as everything else about this haunting brute, whatever it is. I suppose you think this is the print left by the thing which attacked you the night before last?"

"I fancy it is," said Low, who was still bending over the floor eagerly. "What do you make of it, Houston?"

"The brute has only one leg, to start with," replied Houston, "and that leaves the mark of a large, clawless pad! It's some animal--some ghoulish monster!"

"On the contrary," said Low, "I think we have now every reason to conclude that it is a man."

"A man? What man ever left footmarks like these?"

"Look at these hollows and streaks at the sides; they are the traces of the sticks we have heard tapping."

"You don't convince me," returned Hodgson doggedly.

"Let us wait another twenty-four hours, and to-morrow night, if nothing further occurs, I will give you my conclusions. Think it over. The tapping, the bladder, and the fact that Mr. Van Nuysen had lived in Trinidad. Add to these things this single pad-like print. Does nothing strike you by way of a solution?"

Houston shook his head.

"Nothing. And I fail to connect any of these things with what happened both to you and Filderg."

"Ah! now," said Flaxman Low, his face clouding a little, "I confess you lead me into a somewhat different region, though to me the connection is perfect."

Houston raised his eyebrows and laughed.

"If you can unravel this tangle of hints and events and diagnose the ghost, I shall be extremely astonished," he said. "What can you make of the footless impression?"

"Something, I hope. In fact, that mark may be a clue--an outrageous one, perhaps, but still a clue."

That evening the weather broke, and by night the storm had risen to a gale, accompanied by sharp bursts of rain.

"It's a noisy night," remarked Houston; "I don't suppose we'll hear the ghost, supposing it does turn up."

This was after dinner, as they were about to go into the smoking-room. Houston, finding the gas low in the hall, stopped to run it higher; at the same time asking Low to see if the jet on the upper landing was also alight.

Flaxman Low glanced up and uttered a slight exclamation, which brought Houston to his side.

Looking down at them from over the banisters was a face--a blotched, yellowish face, flanked by two swollen, protruding ears, the whole aspect being strangely leonine. It was but a glimpse, a clash of meeting glances, as it were, a glare of defiance, and the face was quickly withdrawn as the two men literally leapt up the stairs.

"There's nothing here," exclaimed Houston, after a search had been carried out through every room above.

"I didn't suppose we'd find anything," returned Low.

"This fairly knots up the thread," said Houston. "You can't pretend to unravel it now."

"Come down," said Low briefly; "I'm ready to give you my opinion, such as it is."

Once in the smoking-room, Houston busied himself in turning on all the light he could procure, then he saw to securing the windows, and piled up an immense fire, while Flaxman Low, who, as usual, had a cigarette in his mouth, sat on the edge of the table and watched him with some amusement.

"You saw that abominable face?" cried Houston, as he threw himself into a chair. "It was as material as yours or mine. But where did he go to? He must be somewhere about."

"We saw him clearly. That is sufficient for our purpose."

"You are very good at enumerating points, Low. Now just listen to my list. The difficulties grow with every fresh discovery. We're at a deadlock now, I take it? The sticks and the tapping point to an old man, the playing with a bladder to a child; the footmark might be the pad of a tiger minus claws, yet the thing that attacked you at night was cold and pulpy. And, lastly, by way of a wind-up, we see a lion-like, human face! If you can make all these items square with each other, I'll be happy to hear what you have got to say."

"You must first allow me to ask you a question. I understood you to say that no blood relationship existed between you and old Mr. Van Nuysen?"

"Certainly not. He was quite an outsider," answered Houston brusquely.

"In that case you are welcome to my conclusions. All the things you have mentioned point to one explanation. This house is haunted by the ghost of Mr. Van Nuysen, and he was a leper."

Houston stood up and stared at his companion.

"What a horrible notion! I must say I fail to see how you have arrived at such a conclusion."

"Take the chain of evidence in rather different order," said Low. "Why should a man tap with a stick?"

"Generally because he's blind."

"In cases of blindness, one stick is used for guidance. Here we have two for support."

"A man who has lost the use of his feet."

"Exactly; a man who has from some cause partially lost the use of his feet."

"But the bladder and the lion-like face?" went on Houston.

"The bladder, or what seemed to us to resemble a bladder, was one of his feet, contorted by the disease and probably swathed in linen, which foot he dragged rather than used; consequently, in passing through a door, for example, he would in the habit of drawing it in after him. Now, as regards the single footmark we saw. In one form of leprosy, the smaller bones of the extremities frequently fall away. The pad-like impression was, as I believe, the mark of the other foot--a toeless foot which he used, because in a more advanced stage of the disease the maimed hand or foot heals and becomes callous."

"Go on," said Houston; "it sounds as if it might be true. And the lion-like face I can account for myself. I have been in China, and have seen it before in lepers."

"Mr. Van Nuysen had been in Trinidad for many years, as we know, and while there he probably contracted the disease."

"I suppose so. After his return," added Houston, "he shut himself up almost entirely, and gave out that he was a martyr to rheumatic gout, this awful thing being the true explanation."

"It also accounts for Mrs. Van Nuysen's determination not to return to her husband."

Houston appeared much disturbed.

"We can't drop it here, Low," he said, in a constrained voice. "There is a good deal more to be cleared up yet. Can you tell me more?"

"From this point I find myself on less certain ground," replied Low unwillingly. "I merely offer a suggestion, remember--I don't ask you to accept it. I believe Mrs. Van Nuysen was murdered!"

"What?" exclaimed Houston. "By her husband?"

"Indications tend that way."

"But, my good fellow---"

"He suffocated her and then made away with himself. It is a pity that his body was not recovered. The condition of the remains would be the only really satisfactory test of my theory. If the skeleton could even now be found, the fact that he was a leper would be finally settled."

There was a prolonged pause until Houston put another question.

"Wait a minute, Low," he said. "Ghosts are admittedly immaterial. In this instance our spook has an extremely palpable body. Surely this is rather unusual? You have made everything else more or less plain. Can you tell me why this dead leper should have tried to murder you and old Filderg? And also how he came to have the actual physical power to do so?"

Low removed his cigarette to look thoughtfully at the end of it. "Now I lapse into the purely theoretical," he answered. "Cases have been known where the assumption of diabolical agency is apparently justifiable."

"Diabolical agency?--I don't follow you."

"I will try to make myself clear, though the subject is still in a stage of vagueness and immaturity. Van Nuysen committed a murder of exceptional atrocity, and afterwards killed himself. Now, bodies of suicides are known to be peculiarly susceptible to spiritual influences, even to the point of arrested corruption. Add to this our knowledge that the highest aim of an evil spirit is to gain possession of a material body. If I carried out my theory to its logical conclusion, I should say that Van Nuysen's body is hidden somewhere on these premises--that this body is intermittently animated by some spirit, which at certain points is forced to re-enact the gruesome tragedy of the Van Nuysens. Should any living person chance to occupy the position of the first victim, so much the worse for him!"

For some minutes Houston made no remark on this singular expression of opinion.

"But have you ever met with anything of the sort before?" he said at last.

"I can recall," replied Flaxman Low thoughtfully, "quite a number of cases which would seem to bear out this hypothesis. Among them a curious problem of haunting exhaustively examined by Busner in the early part of 1888, at which I was myself lucky enough to assist. Indeed, I may add that the affair which I have recently engaged upon in Vienna offers some rather similar features. There, however, we had to stop short of excavation, by which alone any specific results might have been attained."

"Then you are of the opinion," said Houston, "that pulling the house to pieces might cast some further light upon this affair?"

"I cannot see any better course," said Mr. Low.

Then Houston closed the discussion by a very definite declaration.

"This house shall come down!"

So "The Spaniards" was pulled down.

Such is the story of "The Spaniards," Hammersmith, and it has been given the first place in this series because, although it may not be of so strange a nature as some that will follow it, yet it seems to us to embody in a high degree the peculiar methods by which Mr. Flaxman Low is wont to approach these cases.

The work of demolition, begun at the earliest possible moment, did not occupy very long, and during its early stages, under the boarding at an angle of the landing was found a skeleton. Several of the phalanges were missing, and other indications also established beyond a doubt the fact that the remains were the remains of a leper.

The skeleton is now in the museum of one of our city hospitals. It bears a scientific ticket, and is the only evidence extant of the correctness of Mr. Flaxman Low's methods and the possible truth of his extraordinary theories.

The Story of the Moor Road

"The medical profession must always have its own peculiar off-shoots," said Mr. Flaxman Low, "some are trades, some mere hobbies, others, again, are allied subjects of a serious and profound nature. Now, as a student of psychical phenomena, I account myself only two degrees removed from the ordinary general practitioner."

"How do you make that out?" returned Colonel Daimley, pushing the decanter of old port invitingly across the table.

"The nerve and brain specialist is the link between myself and the man you would send for if you had a touch of lumbago," replied Low with a slight smile. "Each division is but a higher grade of the same ladder—a step upwards into the unknown. I consider that I stand just one step above the specialist who makes a study of brain disease and insanity; he is at work on the disorders of the embodied spirit, while I deal with abnormal conditions of the free and detached spirit."

Colonel Daimley laughed aloud.

"That won't do, Low! No, no! First prove that your ghosts are sick."

"Certainly," replied Low gravely. "A very small proportion of spirits return as apparitions after the death of the body. Hence we may conclude that a ghost is a spirit in an abnormal condition. Abnormal conditions of the body usually indicate disease; why not of the spirit also?"

"That sounds fair enough," observed Lane Chaddam, the third man present. "Has the Colonel told you of our spook?"

The Colonel shook his handsome grey head in some irritation.

"You haven't convinced me yet, Lane, that it is a spook," he said drily. "Human nature is at the bottom of most things in this world according to my opinion."

"What spook is this?" asked Flaxman Low. "I heard nothing of it when I was down with you last year."

"It's a recent acquisition," replied Lane Chaddam. "I wish we were rid of it for my part."

"Have you seen it?" asked Low as he relit his long German pipe.

"Yes, and felt it!"

"What is it?"

"That's for you to say. He nearly broke my neck for me—that's all I can swear to."

Low knew Chaddam well. He was a long-limbed, athletic young fellow, with a good show of cups in his rooms, and was one of the various short-distance runners mentioned in the Badminton as having done the hundred in level time, and not the sort of man whose neck is easy to break.

"How did it happen?" asked Flaxman Low.

"About a fortnight ago," replied Chaddam. "I was flight-shooting near the burn where the hounds killed the otter last year. When the light began to fail, I thought I would come home by the old quarry, and pot anything that showed itself. As I walked along the far bank of the burn, I saw a man on the near side standing on the patch of sand below the reeds and watching me. As I came nearer I heard him coughing; it sounded like a sick cow. He stood still as if waiting for me. I thought it odd, because amongst the meres and water-meadows down there one never meets a stranger."

"Could you see him pretty clearly?"

"I saw his outline clearly, but not his face, because his back was toward the west. He was tall and jerry-built, so to speak, and had a little head no bigger than a child's, and he wore a fur cap with queer upstanding ears. When I came close, he suddenly slipped away; he jumped behind a big dyke, and I lost sight of him. But I didn't pay much attention; I had my gun, and I concluded it was a tramp."

"Tramps don't follow men of your size," observed Low with a smile.

"This fellow did, at any rate. When I got across to the spot where he had been standing—the sand is soft there—I looked for his tracks. I knew he was bound to have a big foot of his own considering his height. But there were no footprints!"

"No footprints? You mean it was too dark for you to see them?" broke in Colonel Daimley.

"I am sure I should have seen them had there been any," persisted Chaddam quietly. "Besides, a man can't take a leap as he did without

15

leaving a good hole behind him. The sand was perfectly smooth, because there had been a strong east wind all day. After looking about and seeing no marks, I went on to the top of the knoll above the quarry. After a bit I felt I was followed, though I couldn't see anyone. You remember the thorn bush that overhangs the quarry pool? I stopped there and bent over the edge of the cliff to see if there was anything in the pool. As I stooped I felt a point like a steel puncheon catch me in the small of the back. I kicked off from the quarry wall as well as I could, so as to avoid the broken rocks below, and I just managed to clear them, but I fell into the water with a flop that knocked the wind out of me. However, I held on to the gun, and, after a minute, I climbed to a ledge under the cliff and waited to see what my friend on top would do next. He waited, too. I couldn't see him, but I heard him—he coughed up there in the dusk, the most ghastly noise I ever heard. The Colonel laughs at me, but it was about as nasty a half-hour as I care to have. In the end, I swam out across the pool and got home."

"I laugh at Lane," said the Colonel, " but all the same, it's a bad spot for a fall."

"You say he struck you in the back?" asked Flaxman Low, turning to Chaddam.

"Yes, and his finger was like a steel punch."

"What does Mrs. Daimley say to this affair?" went on Low presently.

"Not a word to my wife or Olivia, my dear Low!" exclaimed Colonel Daimley. "It would frighten them needlessly; besides, there would be an infernal fuss if we wanted to go flighting or anything after dark. I only fear for them, as they often drive into Nerbury by the Moor Road, which passes close by the quarry."

"Do they go in for their letters every evening as they used to do?"

"Just the same. And they won't take Stubbs with them, in spite of advice." The Colonel looked disconsolately at Low. " Women are angels, bless them! But they are the dickens to deal with because they always want to know why?"

"And now, Low, what have you to say about it?" asked Chaddam.

"Have you told me all?"

"Yes. The only other thing is that Livy says she hears someone coughing in the spinney most lights."

"If all is as you say, Chaddam—pardon me, but in cases like this imagination is apt to play an unsuspected part—I should think that you have come upon a unique experience. What you have told me is not to be explained upon the lines of any ordinary theory."

After this they followed the ladies into the drawing-room, where they found Mrs. Daimley immersed in a novel as usual, and Livy looking pretty enough to account for the frequent presence of Lane Chaddam at Low Riddings. He was a distant cousin of the Colonel, and took advantage of his relationship to pay protracted visits to Northumberland.

Some years previous to the date of the above events, Colonel Daimley had bought and enlarged a substantial farmhouse which stood in a dip south of a lonely sweep of Northumbrian moors. It was a land of pale blue skies and far off fringes of black and ragged pine trees.

From the house a lane led over the wind-swept shoulder of the upland down to a hollow spanned by a railway bridge, then up again across the high levels of the moors until at length it lost itself in the outskirts of the little town of Nerbury. This Moor Road was peculiarly lonely; it approached but one cottage the whole way, and ran very nearly over the doorstep of that one—a deserted-looking slip of a place between the railway bridge and the quarry. Beyond the quarry stretched acres of marshland, meadows and reedy meres, all of which had been manipulated with such ability by the Colonel, that the duck shooting on his land was the envy of the neighbourhood.

In spite of its loneliness the Moor Road was much frequented by the Daimleys, who preferred it to the high road, which was uninteresting and much longer. Mrs. Daimley and Olivia drove in of an evening to fetch their letters—being people with nothing on earth to do, they were naturally always in a hurry to get their letters—and they perpetually had parcels waiting for them at the station which required to be called for at all sorts of hours. Thus it will be seen that the fact of the quarry being haunted by Lane Chaddam's assailant, formed a very real danger to the inhabitants of Low Riddings.

At breakfast next day Livy said the tramp had been coughing in the spinney half the night.

"In what direction?" asked Flaxman Low.

Livy pointed to the window which looked on to the gate and the thick boundary hedge, the last still full of crisp ruddy leaves.

"You feel an interest in your tramp, Miss Daimley?"

"Of course, poor creature! I wanted to go out to look for him the other night, but they would not allow me."

"That was before we knew he was so interesting," said Chaddam. "I promise we'll catch him for you next time he comes."

And this was in fact the programme they tried to carry out, but although the coughing was heard in the spinney, no one even caught a glimpse of any living thing moving or hiding among the trees.

The next stage of the affair happened to be an experience of Livy. In some excitement she told the assembled family at dinner that she had had just seen the coughing tramp.

Lane Chaddam changed colour. "You don't mean to say, Livy, that you went to search for him alone?" he exclaimed half-angrily.

Flaxman Low and the Colonel wisely went on eating oyster patties without taking any apparent notice of the girl's news.

"Why shouldn't I?" asked Livy quickly, " but as it happens I saw him in Scully's cottage by the quarry this evening."

"What?" exclaimed Colonel Daimley, "in Scully's cottage. I'll see to that."

"Why? Are you all so prejudiced against my poor tramp?"

"On the contrary," replied Flaxman Low, "we all want to know what he's like."

"So odd-looking! I was driving home alone from the post when, as I passed the quarry cottage, I heard the cough. You know it is quite unmistakable; I looked up at the window and there he was. I have never seen anybody in the least like him. His face is ghastly pale and perfectly hairless, and he has such a little head. He stared at me so threateningly that I whipped up Lorelie."

"Were you frightened, then?"

"Not exactly, but he had such a wicked face that I drove away as fast as I could."

"I understood that you had arranged to send Stubbs for the letters?" said Colonel Daimley with some annoyance. "Why can't girls say what they mean?"

Livy made no reply, and after a pause Chaddam put a question.

"You must have passed along the Moor Road about seven o'clock?"

"Yes, it was after six when I left the Post-Office," replied Livy. "Why?"

"It was quite dark—how did you see the hairless man so plainly? I was round on the marshes all the evening, and I am quite certain there was no light at any time in Scully's cottage."

"I don't remember whether there was any light behind him in the room," returned Livy after a moment's consideration; "I only know that I saw his head and face quite plainly."

There was no more said on the subject at the time, though the Colonel forbade Livy to run any further risks by going alone on the Moor Road. After this, the three men paraded the lane and lay in wait for the hairless tramp or ghost. On the second evening their watch was rewarded, when Chaddam came hurriedly into the smoking-room to say that the coughing could at that instant be heard in the hedge by the dining-room. It was still early, although the evening had closed in with clouds, and all outside was dark.

"I'll deal with him this time effectually!" exclaimed the Colonel. "I'll slip out the back way, and lie in the hedge down the road by the field gate. You two must chivy him out to me, and when he comes along, I'll have him against the sky-line and give him a charge of No. 4 if he shows fight."

The Colonel stole down the lane while the others beat the spinney and hedge, Flaxman Low very much chagrined at being forced to deal with an interesting problem in this rough and ready fashion. However, he saw that on this occasion at least it would be useless to oppose the Colonel's notions. When he and Chaddam met after beating the hedge they saw a tall figure shamble away rapidly down the lane towards the Colonel's hiding-place.

They stood still and waited for developments, but the minutes followed each other in intense stillness. Then they went to find the Colonel.

"Hullo, Colonel, anything wrong?" asked Chaddam on nearing the field gate.

The Colonel straightened himself with the help of Chaddam's arm.

"Did you see him?" he whispered.

"We thought so. Why did you not fire?"

"Because," said the Colonel in a husky voice, "I had no gun!"

"But you took it with you?"

"Yes."

Flaxman Low opened the lantern he carried, and, as the light swept round in a wide circle, something glinted on the grass. It was the stock of the Colonel's gun. A little further off they came upon the Damascus barrels bent and twisted into a ball like so much fine wire. Presently the Colonel explained.

"I saw him coming and meant to meet him, but I seemed dazed—I couldn't move! The gun was snatched from me, and I made no resistance—I don't know why." He took the gunbarrels and examined them slowly, "I give in. Low, no human hand did that."

"During dinner Flaxman Low said abruptly: "I suspect you have lately had an earthquake down here."

"How did you know?" asked Livy. "Have you been to the quarry?"

Low said he had not.

"It was such a poor little earthquake that even the papers did not think it worth while to mention it!" went on Livy. "We didn't feel any shock, and, in fact, knew nothing about it until Dr. Petterped told us."

"You had a landslip though?" went on Low.

Livy opened her pretty eyes.

"But you know all about it," she said. "Yes, the landslip was just by the old quarry."

"I should like to see the place to-morrow," observed Low.

Next day, therefore, when the Colonel went off to the coverts with a couple of neighbours, whom he had invited to join him, Flaxman Low accompanied Chaddam to examine the scene of the landslip.

From the edge of the upland, looking across the hollow crowded with reedy pools, they could see in the torn, reddish flank of the opposite slope the sharp tilt of the broken strata. To the right of this lay the old quarry, and about a hundred yards to the left the lonely house and the curving road.

Low descended into the hollow and spent a long time in the spongy ground between the back of the quarry and the lower edge of the newly-uncovered strata, using his little hammer freely, especially about one narrow black fissure, round which he sniffed and pottered in absorbed silence. Presently he called to Chaddam.

"There has been a slight explosion of gas—a rare gas, here," he said. "I hardly hoped to find traces of it, but it is unmistakeable."

"Very unmistakeable," agreed Chaddam, with a laugh. "You'd have said so had you been here when it happened."

"Ah, very satisfactory indeed. And that was a fortnight ago, you say?"

"Rather more now. It took place a couple of days before my fall into the quarry pool."

"Anyone ill near by—at that cottage for instance?" asked Low, as he joined Chaddam.

"Why? Was that gas poisonous? There's a man in the Colonel's employ named Scully in that cottage, who has had pneumonia, but he was on the mend when the landslip occurred. Since then he has grown steadily worse."

"Is there anyone with him?"

"Yes, the Daimleys sent for a woman to look after him. Scully's a very decent man. I often go in to see him."

"And so does the hairless man apparently," added Low.

"No, that's the queer part of it. Neither he nor the woman in charge have ever seen such a person as Livy described. I don't know what to think."

"The first thing to be done is to get the man from here at once," said Low decidedly. "Let's go in and see him."

They found Scully low and drowsy. The nurse shook her head at the two visitors in a despondent way.

"He grows weaker day by day," she said.

"Get him away from here at once," repeated Low, as they went out.

"We might have him up at Low Riddings, but he seems almost too weak to be moved," replied Chaddam doubtfully.

"My dear fellow, it's his only chance of life."

The Daimleys made arrangements for the reception of Scully, provided Dr. Thomson of Nerbury gave his consent to the removal. In the afternoon, therefore, Chaddam bicycled into Nerbury to see the doctor on the subject. "If were you, Chaddam," said Low before he started, "I'd be back by daylight."

Unfortunately Dr. Thomson was on his rounds, and did not return until after dark, by which time it was too late to remove Scully that evening. After leaving the doctor's house Chaddam went to the station to inquire about a box from Mudie's. The books having arrived, he took out a couple of volumes for Mrs. Daimley's present consumption, and was strapping them on in front of his bicycle, when it struck him that unless he went home by the Moor Road he would be late for dinner.

Accordingly he branched off into the bare track which led over the moors. The twilight had deepened into a fine, cold night, and a moon was swinging up into a pale, clear sky. The spread of heather, purple in the daytime, appeared jet black by moonlight, and across it he could see the white ribbon of road stretching ahead into the distance. The scents of the night were fresh in his nostrils, as he ran easily along the level with the breeze behind him.

He soon reached the incline past Scully's cottage. Well away to the left lay the quarry pool like a blotch of ink under its shadowing cliff. There was no light in the cottage, and it seemed even more deserted-looking than usual.

As Chaddam flashed under the bridge, he heard a cough, and glanced back over his shoulder.

A tall, loose-jointed form he had seen once before, was rearing itself up upon the railway bridge. There was something curiously unhuman about the lank outlines and the cant of the small head with its prick-eared cap showing out so clearly against the lighter sky behind.

When Chaddam looked again, he saw the thing on the bridge fling up its long arms and leap down on to the road some thirty feet below.

Then Chaddam rode. He began to think he had been a fool to come, and he counted that he was a good mile from home. At first he fancied he heard footfalls, then he fancied there were none. The hard road flew under him, all thoughts of economising his strength were lost, his single aim was to make the pace.

Suddenly his bicycle jerked violently, and he was shot over into the road. As he fell, he turned his head and was conscious of a little, bleached, bestial face, wet with fury, not ten yards behind!

He sprang to his feet, and ran up the road as he had never run before. He ran wonderfully, but he might as well have tried to race a cheetah. It was not a question of speed, the game was in the hands of this thing with the limbs of a starved Hercules, whose bony knees seemed to leap into its ghastly face at every stride. Chaddam topped the slope with a sickening sense of his own powerlessness. Already he saw Low Riddings in the distance, and a dim light came creeping along the road towards him. Another frantic spurt, and he had almost reached the light, when a hand closed like a vice on his shoulder, and seemed to fasten on the flesh. He rushed blindly on towards the house. He saw the door-handle gleam, and in another second he had pitched head foremost on to the knotted matting in the hall.

When he recovered his senses, his first question was: "Where is Low?"

"Didn't you meet him?" asked Livy, " I—that is, we were anxious about you as you were so late, and I was just going to meet you when Mr. Low came downstairs and insisted on going instead."

Chaddam stood up.

"I must follow him."

But as he spoke the front door opened, and Flaxman Low entered, and looked up at the clock.

"Eight-twenty," he said, "You're late, Chaddam."

Afterwards in the smoking-room he gave an account of what he had seen.

"I saw Chaddam racing up the road with a tall figure behind him. It stretched out its hand and grasped his shoulder. The next instant it stopped short as if it had been shot. It seemed to reel back and collapse, and then limped off into the hedge like a disappointed dog."

Chaddam stood up and began to take off his coat.

"Whatever the thing is, it is something out of the common. Look here!" he said, turning up his shirtsleeve over the point of his shoulder, where three singular marks were visible, irregularly placed as the fingers of a hand might fall. They were oblong in shape, about the size of a bean, and swollen in purple lumps well above the surface of the skin.

"Looks as if someone had been using a small cupping glass on you," remarked the Colonel uneasily. "What do you say to it, Low?"

"I say that since Chaddam has escaped with his life, I have only to congratulate him on what, in Europe certainly, is a unique adventure."

The Colonel threw his cigar into the fire.

"Such adventures are too dangerous for my taste," he said. "This creature has on two occasions murderously attacked Lane Chaddam, and it would, no doubt, have attacked Livy if it had had the chance. We must leave this place at once, or we shall be murdered in our beds!"

"I don't think, Colonel, that you will be troubled with this mysterious visitant again, replied Flaxman Low.

"Why not? Who or what is this horrible thing?"

"I believe it to be an Elemental Earth Spirit," returned Low. "No other solution fits the facts of the case."

"What is an Elemental?" resumed the Colonel irritably. "Remember, Low, I expect you to prove your theories so that a plain man may understand, if I am to stay on at Low Riddings."

"Eastern occultists describe wandering tribes of earth spirits, evil intelligences, possessing spirit as distinct from soul—all inimical to man."

"But how do you know that the thing on the Moor Road is an Elemental?"

"Because the points of resemblance are curiously remarkable. The occultists say that when these spirits materialize, they appear in grotesque and uncouth forms; secondly, that they are invariably bloodless and hairless; thirdly, they move with extraordinary rapidity, and leave no footprints; and, lastly, their agility and strength is superhuman. All these peculiarities have been observed in connection with the figure on the Moor Road."

"I admit that no man I have ever met with," commented Colonel Daimley, "could jump uninjured from a height of 30ft., race a bicycle, and twist up gunbarrels like so much soft paper. So perhaps you're right. But can you tell me why or how it came here?"

"My conclusions," began Low, "may seem to you far-fetched and ridiculous, but you must give them the benefit of the fact that they precisely account for the otherwise unaccountable features which mark this affair. I connect this appearance with the earthquake and the sick man."

"What? Scully in league with the devil?" exclaimed the Colonel bluntly. "Why the man is too weak to leave his bed; besides, he is a short, thick-set fellow, entirely unlike our haunting friend."

"You mistake me, Colonel," said Low, in his quiet tones. "These Elementals cannot take form without drawing upon the resources of the living. They absorb the vitality of any ailing person until it is exhausted, and the person dies."

"Then they begin operations upon a fresh victim? A pleasant lookout to know we keep a well-attested vampire in the neighbourhood!"

"Vampires are a distinct race, with different methods; one being that the Elemental is a wanderer, and goes far afield to search for a new victim."

"But why should it want to kill me?" put in Chaddam.

"As I have told you, they are animated solely by a blind malignity to the human race, and you happened to be handy."

"But the earthquake, Low; where is the connection there?" demanded the Colonel, with the air of a man who intends to corner his opponent.

Flaxman Low lit one cigar at the end of another before he replied.

"At this point," he said, "my own theories and observations and those of the old occultists overlap. The occultists held that some of these spirits are imprisoned in the interior of the earth, but may be set free in consequence of those shiftings and disturbances which take place during an earthquake. This in more modern language simply means that Elementals are in some manner connected with certain of the primary strata. Now, my own researches have led me to conclude that atmospheric influences are intimately associated with spiritual phenomena. Some gases appear to be productive of such phenomena. One of these is generated when certain of the primary formations are newly exposed to the common air."

"This is almost beyond belief—I don't understand you," said the Colonel.

"I am sorry that I cannot give you all the links in my own chain of reasoning," returned Low. "Much is still obscure, but the evidence is sufficiently strong to convince me that in such a case of earthquake and landslip as has lately taken place here the phenomenon of an embodied Elemental might possibly be expected to follow, given the one necessary adjunct of a sick person in the near neighbourhood of the disturbance."

"But when this brute got hold of me, why didn't it finish me off?" asked Chaddam. "Or was it your coming that prevented it?"

Flaxman Low considered.

"No, I don't think I can flatter myself that my coming had anything to do with your escape. It was a near thing—how near you will understand when we hear further news of Scully in the morning."

A servant entered the room at this moment.

"The woman has come up from the cottage, sir, to say that Scully is dead."

"At what hour did he die?" asked Low.

"About ten minutes past eight, sir, she says."

"The hour agrees exactly," commented Low, when the man had left the room. "The figure stopped and collapsed so suddenly that I believed something of this kind must have happened."

"But surely this is a very unprecedented occurrence?"

"It is," said Flaxman Low. "But I can assure you that if you take the trouble to glance through the pages of the psychical periodicals you will find many statements at least as wonderful."

"But are they true?"

"At any rate," said he, "we know this is."

The Daimleys have spent many pleasant days at Low Riddings since then, but Chaddam—who has acquired a right to control Miss Livy's actions more or less—persists in his objection to any solitary expeditions to Nerbury along the Moor Road. For, although the figure has never been seen about Low Riddings since, some strange stories have lately appeared in the papers of a similar mysterious figure which has been met with more than once in the lonelier spots about North London. If it be true that this nameless wandering spirit, with the strength and activity of twenty men, still haunts our lonely roads, the sooner Mr. Flaxman Low exorcises it the better.

The Story of Baelbrow

It is a matter for regret that so many of Mr Flaxman Low's reminiscences should deal with the darker episodes of his experiences. Yet this is almost unavoidable, as the more purely scientific and less strongly marked cases would not, perhaps, contain the same elements of interest for the general public, however valuable and instructive they might be to the expert student. It has also been considered better to choose the completer cases, those that ended in something like satisfactory proof, rather than the many instances where the thread broke off abruptly amongst surmisings, which it was never possible to subject to convincing tests.

North of a low-lying strip of country on the East Anglian coast, the promontory of Bael Ness thrusts out a blunt nose into the sea. On the Ness, backed by pinewoods, stands a square, comfortable stone mansion, known to the countryside as Baelbrow. It has faced the east winds for close upon three hundred years, and during the whole period has been the home of the Swaffam family, who were never in anywise put out of conceit of their ancestral dwelling by the fact that it had always been haunted. Indeed, the Swaffams were proud of the Baelbrow Ghost, which enjoyed a wide notoriety, and no one dreamt of complaining of its behaviour until Professor Van der Voort of Louvain laid information against it, and sent an urgent appeal for help to Mr Flaxman Low.

The Professor, who was well acquainted with Mr Low, detailed the circumstances of his tenancy of Baelbrow, and the unpleasant events that had followed thereupon.

It appeared that Mr Swaffam, senior, who spent a large portion of his time abroad, had offered to lend his house to the Professor for the summer season. When the Van der Voorts arrived at Baelbrow, they were charmed with the place. The prospect, though not very varied, was at least extensive, and the air exhilarating. Also the Professor's daughter enjoyed frequent visits from her betrothed--Harold Swaffam--and the Professor was delightfully employed in overhauling the Swaffam library.

The Van der Voorts had been duly told of the ghost, which lent distinction to the old house, but never in any way interfered with the comfort of the inmates. For some time they found this description to be strictly true, but with the beginning of October came a change. Up to this time and as far back as the Swaffam annals reached, the ghost had been a shadow, a rustle, a passing sigh--nothing definite or troublesome. But early in October strange things began to occur, and the terror culminated when a housemaid was found dead in a corridor three weeks later. Upon this the Professor felt that it was time to send for Flaxman Low.

Mr Low arrived upon a chilly evening when the house was already beginning to blur in the purple twilight, and the resinous scent of the pines came sweetly on the land breeze. Van der Voort welcomed him in the spacious, fire-lit hall. He was a stout man with a quantity of white hair, round eyes emphasised by spectacles, and a kindly, dreamy face. His life-study was philology, and his two relaxations chess and the smoking of a big bowled meerschaum.

'Now, Professor,' said Mr Low when they had settled themselves in the smoking-room, 'how did it all begin?'

'I will tell you,' replied Van der Voort, thrusting out his chin, and tapping his broad chest, and speaking as if an unwarrantable liberty had been taken with him. 'First of all, it has shown itself to me!' Mr Flaxman Low smiled and assured him that nothing could be more satisfactory.

'But not at all satisfactory!' exclaimed the Professor. 'I was sitting here alone, it might have been midnight--when I hear something come creeping like a little dog with its nails, tick-tick, upon the oak flooring of the hall. I whistle, for I think it is the little "Rags" of my daughter, and afterwards opened the door, and I saw'--he hesitated and looked hard at Low through his spectacles, 'something that was just disappearing into the passage which connects the two wings of the house. It was a figure, not unlike the human figure, but narrow and straight. I fancied I saw a bunch of black hair, and a flutter of something detached, which may have been a handkerchief.

I was overcome by a feeling of repulsion. I heard a few clicking steps, then it stopped, as I thought, at the museum door. Come, I will show you the spot.'

27

The Professor conducted Mr Low into the hall. The main staircase, dark and massive, yawned above them, and directly behind it ran the passage referred to by the Professor. It was over twenty feet long, and about midway led past a deep arch containing a door reached by two steps.

Van der Voort explained that this door formed the entrance to a large room called the Museum, in which Mr Swaffam, senior, who was something of a dilettante, stored the various curios he picked up during his excursions abroad. The Professor went on to say that he immediately followed the figure, which he believed had gone into the museum, but he found nothing there except the cases containing Swaffam's treasures.

'I mentioned my experience to no one. I concluded that I had seen the ghost. But two days after, one of the female servants coming through the passage, in the dark, declared that a man leapt out at her from the embrasure of the Museum door, but she released herself and ran screaming into the servants' hall. We at once made a search but found nothing to substantiate her story.

'I took no notice of this, though it coincided pretty well with my own experience. The week after, my daughter Lena came down late one night for a book. As she was about to cross the hall, something leapt upon her from behind. Women are of little use in serious investigations--she fainted! Since then she has been ill and the doctor says "run down".' Here the Professor spread out his hands. 'So she leaves for a change tomorrow. Since then other members of the household have been attacked in much the same manner, with always the same result, they faint and are weak and useless when they recover.

'But, last Wednesday, the affair became a tragedy. By that time the servants had refused to come through the passage except in a crowd of three or four,--most of them preferring to go round by the terrace to reach this part of the house. But one maid, named Eliza Freeman, said she was not afraid of the Baelbrow Ghost, and undertook to put out the lights in the hall one night.

When she had done so, and was returning through the passage past the Museum door, she appears to have been attacked, or at any rate frightened. In the grey of the morning they found her lying beside the steps dead. There was a little blood upon her sleeve but no mark upon her body except a small raised pustule under the ear. The doctor said the girl was extraordinarily anæmic, and that she probably died from fright, her heart being weak. I was surprised at this, for she had always seemed to be a particularly strong and active young woman.'

'Can I see Miss Van der Voort to-morrow before she goes?' asked Low, as the Professor signified he had nothing more to tell.

The Professor was rather unwilling that his daughter should be questioned, but he at last gave his permission, and next morning Low had a short talk with the girl before she left the house. He found her a very pretty girl, though listless and startlingly pale, and with a frightened stare in her light brown eyes. Mr Low asked if she could describe her assailant. 'No,' she answered. 'I could not see him for he was behind me. I only saw a dark, bony hand, with shining nails, and a bandaged arm pass just under my eyes before I fainted.'

'Bandaged arm? I have heard nothing of this.'

'Tut--tut, mere fancy!' put in the Professor impatiently.

'I saw the bandages on the arm,' repeated the girl, turning her head wearily away, 'and I smelt the antiseptics it was dressed with.'

'You have hurt your neck,' remarked Mr Low, who noticed a small circular patch of pink under her ear.

She flushed and paled, raising her hand to her neck with a nervous jerk, as she said in a low voice: 'It has almost killed me. Before he touched me, I knew he was there! I felt it!'

When they left her the Professor apologised for the unreliability of her evidence, and pointed out the discrepancy between her statement and his own.

'She says she sees nothing but an arm, yet I tell you it had no arms! Preposterous! Conceive a wounded man entering this house to frighten the young women! I do not know what to make of it! Is it a man, or is it the Baelbrow Ghost?'

During the afternoon when Mr Low and the Professor returned from a stroll on the shore, they found a dark-browed young man with a bull neck, and strongly marked features, standing sullenly before the hall fire. The Professor presented him to Mr Low as Harold Swaffam.

Swaffam seemed to be about thirty, but was already known as a far-seeing and successful member of the Stock Exchange.

'I am pleased to meet you, Mr Low,' he began, with a keen glance, 'though you don't look sufficiently high-strung for one of your profession.'

Mr Low merely bowed.

'Come, you don't defend your craft against my insinuations?' went on Swaffam. 'And so you have come to rout out our poor old ghost from Baelbrow? You forget that he is an heirloom, a family possession! What's this about his having turned rabid, eh, Professor?' he ended, wheeling round upon Van der Voort in his brusque way.

The Professor told the story over again. It was plain that he stood rather in awe of his prospective son-in-law.

'I heard much the same from Lena, whom I met at the station,' said Swaffam. 'It is my opinion that the women in this house are suffering from an epidemic of hysteria. You agree with me, Mr Low?'

'Possibly. Though hysteria could hardly account for Freeman's death.'

'I can't say as to that until I have looked further into the particulars. I have not been idle since I arrived. I have examined the Museum. No one has entered it from the outside, and there is no other way of entrance except through the passage. The flooring is laid, I happen to know, on a thick layer of concrete. And there the case for the ghost stands at present.' After a few moments of dogged reflection, he swung round on Mr Low, in a manner that seemed peculiar to him when about to address any person. 'What do you say to this plan, Mr Low? I propose to drive the Professor over to Ferryvale, to stop there for a day or two at the hotel, and I will also dispose of the servants who still remain in the house for, say, forty-eight hours. Meanwhile you and I can try to go further into the secret of the ghost's new pranks?'

Flaxman Low replied that this scheme exactly met his views, but the Professor protested against being sent away. Harold Swaffam, however, was a man who liked to arrange things in his own fashion, and within forty-five minutes he and Van der Voort departed in the dogcart. The evening was lowering, and Baelbrow, like all houses built in exposed situations, was extremely susceptible to the changes of the weather. Therefore, before many hours were over, the place was full of creaking noises as the screaming gale battered at the shuttered windows, and the tree-branches tapped and groaned against the walls.

Harold Swaffam on his way back was caught in the storm and drenched to the skin. It was, therefore, settled that after he had changed his clothes he should have a couple of hours' rest on the smoking-room sofa, while Mr Low kept watch in the hall.

The early part of the night passed over uneventfully. A light burned faintly in the great wainscotted hall, but the passage was dark. There was nothing to be heard but the wild moan and whistle of the wind coming in from the sea, and the squalls of rain dashing against the windows.

As the hours advanced, Mr Low lit a lantern that lay at hand, and, carrying it along the passage tried the Museum door. It yielded, and the wind came muttering through to meet him. He looked round at the shutters and behind the big cases which held Mr Swaffam's treasures, to make sure that the room contained no living occupant but himself.

Suddenly he fancied he heard a scraping noise behind him, and turned round, but discovered nothing to account for it. Finally, he laid the lantern on a bench so that its light should fall through the door into the passage, and returned again to the hall, where he put out the lamp, and then once more took up his station by the closed door of the smoking-room.

A long hour passed, during which the wind continued to roar down the wide hall chimney, and the old boards creaked as if furtive footsteps were gathering from every corner of the house. But Flaxman Low heeded none of these; he was awaiting for a certain sound.

After a while, he heard it--the cautious scraping of wood on wood. He leant forward to watch the Museum door. Click, click, came the curious dog-like tread upon the tiled floor of the Museum, till the thing, whatever it was, paused and listened behind the open door. The wind lulled at the moment, and Low listened also, but no further sound was to be heard, only slowly across the broad ray of light falling through the door grew a stealthy shadow.

Again the wind rose, and blew in heavy gusts about the house, till even the flame in the lantern flickered; but when it steadied once more, Flaxman Low saw that the silent form had passed through the door, and was now on the steps outside. He could just make out a dim shadow in the dark angle of the embrasure.

Presently, from the shapeless shadow came a sound Mr Low was not prepared to hear. The thing sniffed the air with the strong, audible inspiration of a bear, or some large animal. At the same moment, carried on the draughts of the hall, a faint, unfamiliar odour reached his nostrils.

Lena Van der Voort's words flashed back upon him--this, then, was the creature with the bandaged arm!

Again, as the storm shrieked and shook the windows, a darkness passed across the light. The thing had sprung out from the angle of the door, and Flaxman Low knew that it was making its way towards him through the illusive blackness of the hall. He hesitated for a second; then he opened the smoking-room door.

Harold Swaffam sat up on the sofa, dazed with sleep. 'What has happened? Has it come?'

Low told him what he had just seen. Swaffam listened half-smilingly.

'What do you make of it now?' he said.

'I must ask you to defer that question for a little,' replied Low.

'Then you mean me to suppose that you have a theory to fit all these incongruous items?'

'I have a theory, which may be modified by further knowledge,' said Low. 'Meantime, am I right in concluding from the name of this house that it was built on a barrow or burying-place?'

'You are right, though that has nothing to do with the latest freaks of our ghost,' returned Swaffam decidedly.

'I also gather that Mr Swaffam has lately sent home one of the many cases now lying in the Museum?' went on Mr Low.

'He sent one, certainly, last September.'

'And you have opened it,' asserted Low.

'Yes; though I flattered myself I had left no trace of my handiwork.'

'I have not examined the cases,' said Low. 'I inferred that you had done so from other facts.'

'Now, one thing more,' went on Swaffam, still smiling. 'Do you imagine there is any danger---I mean to men like ourselves? Hysterical women cannot be taken into serious account.'

'Certainly; the gravest danger to any person who moves about this part of the house alone after dark,' replied Low.

Harold Swaffam leant back and crossed his legs.

'To go back to the beginning of our conversation, Mr Low, may I remind you of the various conflicting particulars you will have to reconcile before you can present any decent theory to the world?'

'I am quite aware of that.'

'First of all, our original ghost was a mere misty presence, rather guessed at from vague sounds and shadows--now we have a something that is tangible, and that can, as we have proof, kill with fright. Next Van der Voort declares the thing was a narrow, long and distinctly armless object, while Miss Van der Voort has not only seen the arm and hand of a human being, but saw them clearly enough to tell us that the nails were gleaming and the arm bandaged. She also felt its strength. Van der Voort, on the other hand, maintained that it clicked along like a dog--you bear out this description with the additional information that it sniffs like a wild beast. Now what can this thing be? It is capable of being seen, smelt, and felt, yet it hides itself, successfully in a room where there is no cavity or space sufficient to afford covert to a cat! You still tell me that you believe that you can explain?'

'Most certainly,' replied Flaxman Low with conviction.

'I have not the slightest intention or desire to be rude, but as a mere matter of common sense, I must express my opinion plainly. I believe the whole thing to be the result of excited imaginations, and I am about to prove it. Do you think there is any further danger to-night?'

'Very great danger to-night,' replied Low.

'Very well; as I said, I am going to prove it. I will ask you to allow me to lock you up in one of the distant rooms, where I can get no help from you, and I will pass the remainder of the night walking about the passage and hall in the dark. That should give proof one way or the other.'

'You can do so if you wish, but I must at least beg to be allowed to look on. I will leave the house and watch what goes on from the window in the passage, which I saw opposite the Museum door. You cannot, in any fairness, refuse to let me be a witness.'

'I cannot, of course,' returned Swaffam. 'Still, the night is too bad to turn a dog out into, and I warn you that I shall lock you out.'

'That will not matter. Lend me a macintosh, and leave the lantern lit in the Museum, where I placed it.'

Swaffam agreed to this. Mr Low gives a graphic account of what followed. He left the house and was duly locked out, and, after groping his way round the house, found himself at length outside the window of the passage, which was almost opposite to the door of the Museum. The door was still ajar and a thin band of light cut out into the gloom. Further down the hall gaped black and void. Low, sheltering himself as well as he could from the rain, waited for Swaffam's appearance. Was the terrible yellow watcher balancing itself upon its lean legs in the dim corner opposite, ready to spring out with its deadly strength upon the passer-by? Presently Low heard a door bang inside the house, and the next moment Swaffam appeared with a candle in his hand, an isolated spread of weak rays against the vast darkness behind. He advanced steadily down the passage, his dark face grim and set, and as he came Mr Low experienced that tingling sensation, which is so often the forerunner of some strange experience.

Swaffam passed on towards the other end of the passage. There was a quick vibration of the Museum door as a lean shape with a shrunken head leapt out into the passage after him. Then all together came a hoarse shout, the noise of a fall and utter darkness.

In an instant, Mr Low had broken the glass, opened the window, and swung himself into the passage. There he lit a match and as it flared he saw by its dim light a picture painted for a second upon the obscurity beyond.

Swaffam's big figure lay with outstretched arms, face downwards, and as Low looked a crouching shape extricated itself from the fallen man, raising a narrow vicious head from his shoulder.

The match spluttered feebly and went out, and Low heard a flying step click on the boards, before he could find the candle Swaffam had dropped. Lighting it, he stooped over Swaffam and turned him on his back. The man's strong colour had gone, and the wax-white face looked whiter still against the blackness of hair and brows, and upon his neck under the ear was a little raised pustule, from which a thin line of blood was streaked up to the angle of his cheekbone.

Some instinctive feeling prompted Low to glance up at this moment. Half extended from the Museum doorway were a face and bony neck--a high-nosed, dull-eyed, malignant face, the eye-sockets hollow, and the darkened teeth showing. Low plunged his hand into his pocket, and a shot rang out in the echoing passage-way and hall. The wind sighed through the broken panes, a ribbon of stuff fluttered along the polished flooring, and that was all, as Flaxman Low half dragged, half carried Swaffam into the smoking-room.

It was some time before Swaffam recovered consciousness. He listened to Low's story of how he had found him with a red angry gleam in his sombre eyes.

'The ghost has scored off me,' he said, with an odd, sullen laugh, 'but now I fancy it's my turn! But before we adjourn to the Museum to examine the place, I will ask you to let me hear your notion of things. You have been right in saying there was real danger. For myself I can only tell you that I felt something spring upon me, and I knew no more. Had this not happened I am afraid I should never have asked you a second time what your idea of the matter might be,' he added with a sort of sulky frankness.

'There are two main indications,' replied Low. 'This strip of yellow bandage, which I have just now picked up from the passage floor, and the mark on your neck.'

'What's that you say?' Swaffam rose quickly and examined his neck in a small glass beside the mantelshelf.

'Connect those two, and I think I can leave you to work it out for yourself,' said Low.

'Pray let us have your theory in full,' requested Swaffam shortly.

'Very well,' answered Low good-humouredly--he thought Swaffam's annoyance natural in the circumstances--'The long, narrow figure which seemed to the Professor to be armless is developed on the next occasion. For Miss Van der Voort sees a bandaged arm and a

E. and H. Heron

dark hand with gleaming--which means, of course, gilded--nails. The clicking sound of the footsteps coincides with these particulars, for we know that sandals made of strips of leather are not uncommon in company with gilt nails and bandages. Old and dry leather would naturally click upon your polished floor.'

'Bravo, Mr Low! So you mean to say that this house is haunted by a mummy!'

'That is my idea, and all I have seen confirms me in my opinion.'

'To do you justice, you held this theory before to-night--before, in fact, you had seen anything for yourself. You gathered that my father had sent home a mummy, and you went on to conclude that I had opened the case?'

'Yes. I imagine you took off most of, or rather all, the outer bandages, thus leaving the limbs free, wrapped only in the inner bandages which were swathed round each separate limb. I fancy this mummy was preserved on the Theban method with aromatic spices, which left the skin olive-coloured, dry and flexible, like tanned leather, the features remaining distinct, and the hair, teeth, and eyebrows perfect.'

'So far, good,' said Swaffam. 'But now, how about the intermittent vitality? The postule on the neck of those whom it attacks? And where is our old Baelbrow ghost to come in?'

Swaffam tried to speak in a rallying tone, but his excitement and lowering temper were visible enough, in spite of the attempts he made to suppress them.

'To begin at the beginning,' said Flaxman Low, 'everybody who, in a rational and honest manner, investigates the phenomena of spiritism will, sooner or later, meet in them some perplexing element, which is not to be explained by any of the ordinary theories. For reasons into which I need not now enter, this present case appears to me to be one of these. I am led to believe that the ghost which has for so many years given dim and vague manifestations of its existence in this house is a vampire.'

Swaffam threw back his head with an incredulous gesture.

'We no longer live in the middle ages, Mr Low! And besides, how could a vampire come here?' he said scoffingly.

'It is held by some authorities on these subjects that under certain conditions a vampire may be self-created. You tell me that this house is built upon an ancient barrow, in fact, on a spot where we might naturally expect to find such an elemental psychic germ. In those dead human systems were contained all the seeds for good and evil. The power which causes these psychic seeds or germs to grow is thought,

35

and from being long dwelt on and indulged, a thought might finally gain a mysterious vitality, which could go on increasing more and more by attracting to itself suitable and appropriate elements from its environment. For a long period this germ remained a helpless intelligence, awaiting the opportunity to assume some material form, by means of which to carry out its desires. The invisible is the real; the material only subserves its manifestation.

The impalpable reality already existed, when you provided for it a physical medium for action by unwrapping the mummy's form. Now, we can only judge of the nature of the germ by its manifestation through matter. Here we have every indication of a vampire intelligence touching into life and energy the dead human frame. Hence the mark on the neck of its victims, and their bloodless and anæmic condition. For a vampire, as you know, sucks blood.'

Swaffam rose, and took up the lamp.

'Now, for proof,' he said bluntly. 'Wait a second, Mr Low. You say you fired at this appearance?' And he took up the pistol which Low had laid down on the table.

'Yes, I aimed at a small portion of its foot which I saw on the step.'

Without more words, and with the pistol still in his hand, Swaffam led the way to the Museum. The wind howled round the house, and the darkness, which precedes the dawn, lay upon the world, when the two men looked upon one of the strangest sights it has ever been given to men to shudder at.

Half in and half out of an oblong wooden box in a corner of the great room, lay a lean shape in its rotten yellow bandages, the scraggy neck surmounted by a mop of frizzled hair. The toe strap of a sandal and a portion of the right foot had been shot away.

Swaffam, with a working face, gazed down at it, then seizing it by its tearing bandages, he flung it into the box, where it fell into a life-like posture, its wide, moist-lipped mouth gaping up at them.

For a moment Swaffam stood over the thing; then with a curse he raised the revolver and shot into the grinning face again and again with a deliberate vindictiveness. Finally he rammed the thing down into the box, and, clubbing the weapon, smashed the head into fragments with a vicious energy that coloured the whole horrible scene with a suggestion of murder done.

Then, turning to Low, he said: 'Help me to fasten the cover on it.'

'Are you going to bury it?'

'No, we must rid the earth of it,' he answered savagely. 'I'll put it into the old canoe and burn it.'

The rain had ceased when in the daybreak they carried the old canoe down to the shore. In it they placed the mummy case with its ghastly occupant, and piled faggots about it. The sail was raised and the pile lighted, and Low and Swaffam watched it creep out on the ebb-tide, at first a twinkling spark, then a flare and waving fire, until far out to sea the history of that dead thing ended 3000 years after the priests of Armen had laid it to rest in its appointed pyramid.

The Story of Yand Manor House

By Looking through the notes of Mr. Flaxman Low, one sometimes catches through the steel-blue hardness of facts, the pink flush of romance, or more often the black corner of a horror unnameable. The following story may serve as an instance of the latter. Mr. Low not only unravelled the mystery at Yand, but at the same time justified his life-work to M. Thierry, the well-known French critic and philosopher.

At the end of a long conversation, M. Thierry, arguing from his own standpoint as a materialist, had said:

"The factor in the human economy which you call 'soul' cannot be placed."

"I admit that," replied Low. "Yet, when a man dies, is there not one factor unaccounted for in the change that comes upon him? Yes! For though his body still exists, it rapidly falls to pieces, which proves that that has gone which held it together."

The Frenchman laughed, and shifted his ground.

"Well, for my part, I don't believe in ghosts! Spirit manifestations, occult phenomena--is not this the ashbin into which a certain clique shoot everything they cannot understand, or for which they fail to account?"

"Then what should you say to me, Monsieur, if I told you that I have passed a good portion of my life in investigating this particular ashbin, and have been lucky enough to sort a small part of its contents with tolerable success?" replied Flaxman Low.

"The subject is doubtless interesting--but I should like to have some personal experience in the matter," said Thierry dubiously.

"I am at present investigating a most singular case," said Low. "Have you a day or two to spare?"

Thierry thought for a minute or more.

"I am grateful," he replied. "But, forgive me, is it a convincing ghost?"

"Come with me to Yand and see. I have been there once already, and came away for the purpose of procuring information from MSS. to which I have the privilege of access, for I confess that the phenomena at Yand lie altogether outside any former experience of mine."

Low sank back into his chair with his hands clasped behind his head--a favourite position of his--and the smoke of his long pipe curled up lazily into the golden face of an Isis, which stood behind him on a bracket. Thierry, glancing across, was struck by the strange likeness between the faces of the Egyptian goddess and this scientist of the nineteenth century. On both rested the calm, mysterious abstraction of some unfathomable thought. As he looked, he decided.

"I have three days to place at your disposal."

"I thank you heartily," replied Low. "To be associated with so brilliant a logician as yourself in an inquiry of this nature is more than I could have hoped for! The material with which I have to deal is so elusive, the whole subject is wrapped in such obscurity and hampered by so much prejudice, that I can find few really qualified persons who care to approach these investigations seriously. I go down to Yand this evening, and hope not to leave without clearing up the mystery."

"You will accompany me?"

"Most certainly. Meanwhile pray tell me something of the affair."

"Briefly the story is as follows. Some weeks ago I went to Yand Manor House at the request of the owner, Sir George Blackburton, to see what I could make of the events which took place there. All they complain of is the impossibility of remaining in one room--the dining-room."

"What then is he like, this M. le Spook?" asked the Frenchman, laughing.

"No one has ever seen him, or for that matter heard him."

"Then how--"

"You can't see him, nor hear him, nor smell him," went on Low, "but you can feel him and---taste him!"

"Mon Dieu! But this is singular! Is he then of so bad a. flavour?"

"You shall taste for yourself," answered Flaxman Low smiling. "After a certain hour no one can remain in the room, they are simply crowded out."

"But who crowds them out?" asked Thierry.

"That is just what I hope we may discover to-night or tomorrow."

The last train that night dropped Mr. Flaxman Low and his companion at a little station near Yand. It was late, but a trap in waiting soon carried them to the Manor House. The big bulk of the building stood up in absolute blackness before them.

"Blackburton was to have met us, but I suppose he has not yet arrived," said Low. "Hullo! the door is open," he added as he stepped into the hall.

Beyond a dividing curtain they now perceived a light. Passing behind this curtain they found themselves at the end of the long hall, the wide staircase opening up in front of them.

"But who is this?" exclaimed Thierry.

Swaying and stumbling at every step, there tottered slowly down the stairs the figure of a man.

He looked as if he had been drinking, his face was livid, and his eyes sunk into his head.

"Thank Heaven you've come! I heard you outside," he said in a weak voice.

"It's Sir George Blackburton," said Low, as the man lurched forward and pitched into his arms.

They laid him down on the rugs and tried to restore consciousness.

"He has the air of being drunk, but it is not so," remarked Thierry. "Monsieur has had a bad shock of the nerves. See the pulses drumming in his throat."

In a few minutes Blackburton opened his eyes and staggered to his feet.

"Come. I could not remain there alone. Come quickly."

They went rapidly across the hall, Blackburton leading the way down a wide passage to a double-leaved door, which, after a perceptible pause, he threw open, and they all entered together.

On the great table in the centre stood an extinguished lamp, some scattered food, and a big, lighted candle. But the eyes of all three men passed at once to a dark recess beside the heavy, carved chimneypiece, where a rigid shape sat perched on the back of a huge, oak chair.

Flaxman Low snatched up the candle and crossed the room towards it.

On the top of the chair, with his feet upon the arms, sat a powerfully-built young man huddled up. His mouth was open, and his eyes twisted upwards. Nothing further could be seen from below but the ghastly pallor of cheek and throat.

"Who is this?" cried Low. Then he laid his hand gently on the man's knee.

At the touch the figure collapsed in a heap upon the floor, the gaping, set, terrified face turned up to theirs.

"He's dead!" said Low after a hasty examination. "I should say he's been dead some hours."

"Oh, Lord! Poor Batty!" groaned Sir George, who was entirely unnerved. "I'm glad you've come."

"Who is he?" said Thierry, "and what was he doing here?"

"He's a gamekeeper of mine. He was always anxious to try conclusions with the ghost, and last night he begged me to lock him in here with food for twenty-four hours. I refused at first, but then I thought if anything happened while he was in here alone, it would interest you. Who could imagine it would end like this?"

"When did you find him?" asked Low.

"I only got here from my mother's half an hour ago. I turned on the light in the hall and came in here with a candle. As I entered the room, the candle went out, and--and--I think I must be going mad."

"Tell us everything you saw," urged Low.

"You will think I am beside myself; but as the light went out and I sank almost paralysed into an armchair, I saw two barred eyes looking at me!"

"Barred eyes? What do you mean?"

"Eyes that looked at me through thin vertical bars, like the bars of a cage. What's that?"

With a smothered yell Sir George sprang back. He had approached the dead man and declared something had brushed his face.

"You were standing on this spot under the overmantel. I will remain here. Meantime, my dear Thierry, I feel sure you will help Sir George to carry this poor fellow to some more suitable place," said Flaxman Low.

When the dead body of the young gamekeeper had been carried out, Low passed slowly round and about the room. At length he stood under the old carved overmantel, which reached to the ceiling and projected bodily forward in quaint heads of satyrs and animals. One of these on the side nearest the recess represented a griffin with a flanged mouth. Sir George had been standing directly below this at the moment when he felt the touch on his face. Now alone in the dim, wide room, Flaxman Low stood on the same spot and waited. The candle threw its dull yellow rays on the shadows which seemed to gather closer and wait also. Presently a distant door banged, and Low, leaning forward to listen, distinctly felt something on the back of his neck!

He swung round. There was nothing! He searched carefully on all sides, then put his hand up to the griffin's head. Again came the same soft touch, this time upon his hand, as if something had floated past on the air.

This was definite. The griffin's head located it. Taking the candle to examine more closely, Low found four long black hairs depending from the jagged fangs. He was detaching them when Thierry reappeared.

"We must get Sir George away as soon as possible," he said.

"Yes, we must take him away, I fear," agreed Low. "Our investigation must be put off till to-morrow."

On the following day they returned to Yand. It was a large country-house, pretty and old-fashioned, with lattice windows and deep gables, that looked out between tall shrubs and across lawns set with beaupots, where peacocks sunned themselves on the velvet turf. The church spire peered over the trees on one side; and an old wall covered with ivy and creeping plants, and pierced at intervals with arches, alone separated the gardens from the churchyard.

The haunted room lay at the back of the house. It was square and handsome, and furnished in the style of the last century. The oak overmantel reached to the ceiling, and a wide window, which almost filled one side of the room, gave a view of the west door of the church.

Low stood for a moment at the open window looking out at the level sunlight which flooded the lawns and parterres.

"See that door sunk in the church wall to the left?" said Sir George's voice at his elbow. "That is the door of the family vault. Cheerful outlook, isn't it?"

"I should like to walk across there presently," remarked Low.

"What! Into the vault?" asked Sir George, with a harsh laugh. "I'll take you if you like. Anything else I can show you or tell you?"

"Yes. Last night I found this hanging from the griffin's head," said Low, producing the thin wisp of black hair. "It must have touched your cheek as you stood below. Do you know to whom it can belong?"

"It's a woman's hair! No, the only woman who has been in this room to my knowledge for months is an old servant with grey hair, who cleans it," returned Blackburton. "I'm sure it was not here when I locked Batty in."

"It is human hair, exceedingly coarse and long uncut," said Low; "but it is not necessarily a woman's."

"It is not mine at any rate, for I'm sandy; and poor Batty was fair. Good-night; I'll come round for you in the morning."

Presently, when the night closed in, Thierry and Low settled down in the haunted room to await developments. They smoked and talked deep into the night. A big lamp burned brightly on the table, and the surroundings looked homely and desirable.

Thierry made a remark to that effect, adding that perhaps the ghost might see fit to omit his usual visit.

"Experience goes to prove that ghosts have a cunning habit of choosing persons either credulous or excitable to experiment upon," he added.

To M. Thierry's surprise, Flaxman Low agreed with him.

"They certainly choose suitable persons," he said, "that is, not credulous persons, but those whose senses are sufficiently keen to detect the presence of a spirit. In my own investigations, I try to eliminate what you would call the supernatural element. I deal with these mysterious affairs as far as possible on material lines."

"Then what do you say of Batty's death? He died of fright---simply."

"I hardly think so. The manner of his death agrees in a peculiar manner with what we know of the terrible history of this room. He died of fright and pressure combined. Did you hear the doctor's remark? It was significant. He said: 'The indications are precisely those I have observed in persons who have been crushed and killed in a crowd!'"

"That is sufficiently curious, I allow. I see that it is already past two o'clock. I am thirsty; I will have a little seltzer." Thierry rose from his chair, and, going to the side-board, drew a tumblerful from the syphon. "Pah! What an abominable taste!"

"What? The seltzer?"

"Not at all?" returned the Frenchman irritably. "I have not touched it yet. Some horrible fly has flown into my mouth, I suppose. Pah! Disgusting!"

"What is it like?" asked Flaxman Low, who was at the moment. wiping his own mouth with his handkerchief.

"Like? As if some repulsive fungus had burst in the mouth."

"Exactly. I perceive it also. I hope you are about to be convinced."

"What?" exclaimed Thierry, turning his big figure round and staring at Low. "You don't mean As he spoke the lamp suddenly went out.

"Why, then, have you put the lamp out at such a moment?" cried Thierry, "I have not put it out. Light the candle beside you on the table.". Low heard the Frenchman's grunt of satisfaction as he found the candle, then the scratch of a match. It sputtered and went out. Another match and another behaved in the same manner, while Thierry swore freely under his breath.

"Let me have your matches, Monsieur Flaxman; mine are, no doubt damp," he said at last.

Low rose to feel his way across the room. The darkness was dense.

"It is the darkness of Egypt--it may be felt. Where then are you, my dear friend?" he heard Thierry saying, but the voice seemed a long way off.

"I am coming," he answered, "but it's so hard to get along." After Low had spoken the words, their meaning struck him.

He paused and tried to realise in what part of the room he was. The silence was profound, and the growing sense of oppression seemed like a nightmare. Thierry's voice sounded again, faint and receding.

"I am suffocating, Monsieur Flaxman, where are you? I am near the door. Ach!"

A strangling bellow of pain and fear followed, that scarcely reached Low through the thickening atmosphere.

"Thierry, what is the matter with you?" he shouted. "Open the door."

But there was no answer. What had become of Thierry in that hideous, clogging gloom! Was he also dead, crushed in some ghastly fashion against the wall? What was this? The air had become palpable to the touch, heavy, repulsive, with the sensation of cold humid flesh!

Low pushed out his hands with a mad longing to touch a table, a chair, anything but this clammy, swelling softness that thrust itself upon him from every side, baffling him and filling his grasp.

He knew now that he was absolutely alone--struggling against what? His feet were slipping in his wild efforts to feel the floor--the dank flesh was creeping upon his neck, his cheek--his breath came short and labouring as the pressure swung him gently to and fro, helpless, nauseated!

The clammy flesh crowded upon him like the bulk of some fat, horrible creature; then came a stinging pain on the cheek. Low clutched at something--there was a crash and a rush of air---The next sensation of which Mr. Flaxman Low was conscious was one of deathly sickness. He was lying on wet grass, the wind blowing over him, and all the clean, wholesome smells of the open air in his nostrils.

He sat up and looked about him. Dawn was breaking windily in the east, and by its light he saw that he was on the lawn of Yand Manor House. The latticed window of the haunted room above him was open. He tried to remember what had happened. He took stock of himself, in fact, and slowly felt that he still held something clutched in his right hand--something dark-coloured, slender, and twisted. It might have been a long shred of bark or the cast skin of an adder--it was impossible to see in the dim light.

After an interval the recollection of Thierry recurred to him. Scrambling to his feet, he raised himself to the window-sill and looked in. Contrary to his expectation, there was no upsetting of furniture; everything remained in position as when the lamp went out. His own chair and the one Thierry had occupied were just as when they had arisen from them. But there was no sign of Thierry.

Low jumped in by the window. There was the tumbler full of seltzer, and the litter of matches about it. He took up Thierry's box of matches and struck a light. It flared, and he lit the candle with ease. In fact, everything about the room was perfectly normal; all the horrible conditions prevailing but a couple of hours ago had disappeared.

But where was Thierry? Carrying the lighted candle, he passed out of the door, and searched in the adjoining rooms. In one of them, to his relief, he found the Frenchman sleeping profoundly in an armchair.

Low touched his arm. Thierry leapt to his feet, fending off an imaginary blow with his arm.

Then he turned his scared face on Low.

"What! You, Monsieur Flaxman! How have you escaped?"

"I should rather ask you how you escaped," said Low, smiling at the havoc the night's experiences had worked on his friend's looks and spirits.

"I was crowded out of the room against the door. That infernal thing--what was it?--with its damp, swelling flesh, inclosed me!" A shudder of disgust stopped him. "I was a fly in an aspic. I could not move. I sank into the stifling pulp. The air grew thick. I called to you, but your answers became inaudible. Then I was suddenly thrust against the door by a huge hand--it felt like one, at least. I had a struggle for my life, I was all but crushed, and then, I do not know how, I found myself outside the door. I shouted to you in vain. Therefore, as I could not help you, I came here, and--I will confess it, my dear friend--I locked and bolted the door. After some time I went again into the hall and listened; but, as I heard nothing, I resolved to wait until daylight and the return of Sir George."

"That's all right," said Low. "It was an experience worth having."

"But, no! Not for me! I do not envy you your researches into mysteries of this abominable description. I now comprehend perfectly that

Sir George has lost his nerve if he has had to do with this horror. Besides, it is entirely impossible to explain these things."

At this moment they heard Sir George's arrival, and went out to meet him.

"I could not sleep all night for thinking of you!" exclaimed Blackburton on seeing them; "and I came along as soon as it was light. Something has happened."

"But certainly something has happened," cried M. Thierry shaking his head solemnly; "something of the most bizarre, of the most horrible! Monsieur Flaxman, you shall tell Sir George this story. You have been in that accursed room all night, and remain alive to tell the tale!"

As Low came to the conclusion of the story Sir George suddenly exclaimed:

"You have met with some injury to your face, Mr. Low."

Low turned to the mirror. In the now strong light three parallel weals from eye to mouth could be seen.

"I remember a stinging pain like a lash on my cheek. What would you say these marks were caused by, Thierry?" asked Low.

Thierry looked at them and shook his head.

"No one in their senses would venture to offer any explanation of the occurrences of last night," he replied.

"Something of this sort, do you think?" asked Low again, putting down the object he held in his hand on the table.

Thierry took it up and described it aloud.

"A long and thin object of a brown and yellow colour and twisted like a sabre-bladed corkscrew," then he started slightly and glanced at Low.

"It's a human nail, I imagine," suggested Low.

"But no human being has talons of this kind--except, perhaps, a Chinaman of high rank."

"There are no Chinamen about here, nor ever have been, to my knowledge," said Blackburton shortly. "I'm very much afraid that, in spite of all you have so bravely faced, we are no nearer to any rational explanation."

"On the contrary, I fancy I begin to see my way. I believe, after all, that I may be able to convert you, Thierry," said Flaxman Low.

"Convert me?"

"To a belief in the definite aim of my work. But you shall judge for yourself. What do you make of it so far? I claim that you know as much of the matter as I do."

46

"My dear good friend, I make nothing of it," returned Thierry, shrugging his shoulders and spreading out his hands. "Here we have a tissue of unprecedented incidents that can be explained on no theory whatever."

"But this is definite," and Flaxman Low held up the blackened nail.

"And how do you propose to connect that nail with the black hairs--with the eyes that looked through the bars of a cage--the fate of Batty, with its symptoms of death by pressure and suffocation--our experience of swelling flesh, that something which filled and filled the room to the exclusion of all else? How are you going to account for these things by any kind of connected hypothesis?" asked Thierry, with a shade of irony.

"I mean to try," replied Low.

At lunch time Thierry inquired how the theory was getting on.

"It progresses," answered Low. "By the way, Sir George, who lived in this house for some time prior to, say, 1840? He was a man--it may have been a woman, but, from the nature of his studies, I am inclined to think it was a man--who was deeply read in ancient necromancy, Eastern magic, mesmerism, and subjects of a kindred nature. And was he not buried in the vault you pointed out?"

"Do you know anything more about him?" asked Sir George in surprise.

"He was I imagine," went on Flaxman Low reflectively, "hirsute and swarthy, probably a recluse, and suffered from a morbid and extravagant fear of death."

"How do you know all this?"

"I only asked about it. Am I right?"

"You have described my cousin, Sir Gilbert Blackburton, in every particular. I can show you his portrait in another room."

As they stood looking at the painting of Sir Gilbert Blackburton, with his long, melancholy, olive face and thick, black beard, Sir George went on. "My grandfather succeeded him at Yand. I have often heard my father speak of Sir Gilbert, and his strange studies and extraordinary fear of death. Oddly enough, in the end he died rather suddenly, while he was still hale and strong. He predicted his own approaching death, and had a doctor in attendance for a week or two before he died. He was placed in a coffin he had had made on some plan of his own and buried in the vault. His death occurred in 1842 or 1843. If you care to see them I can show you some of his papers, which may interest you."

Mr. Flaxman Low spent the afternoon over the papers. When evening came, he rose from his work with a sigh of content, stretched himself, and joined Thierry and Sir George in the garden.

They dined at Lady Blackburton's, and it was late before Sir George found himself alone with Mr. Flaxman Low and his friend.

"Have you formed any opinion about the thing which haunts the Manor House?" he asked anxiously.

Thierry elaborated a cigarette, crossed his legs, and added: "If you have in truth come to any definite conclusion, pray let us hear it, my dear Monsieur Flaxman."

"I have reached a very definite and satisfactory conclusion," replied Low. "The Manor House is haunted by Sir Gilbert Blackburton, who died, or, rather, who seemed to die, on the 15th of August, 1842."

"Nonsense! The nail fifteen inches long at the least--how do you connect it with Sir Gilbert?" asked Blackburton testily.

"I am convinced that it belonged to Sir Gilbert," Low answered.

"But the long black hair like a woman's?"

"Dissolution in the case of Sir Gilbert was not complete--not consummated, so to speak--as I hope to show you later. Even in the case of dead persons the hair and nails have been known to grow. By a rough calculation as to the growth of nails in such cases, I was enabled to indicate approximately the date of Sir Gilbert's death. The hair too grew on his head."

"But the barred eyes? I saw them myself!" exclaimed the young man.

"The eyelashes grow also. You follow me?"

"You have, I presume, some theory in connection with this?" observed Thierry. "It must be a very curious one."

"Sir Gilbert in his fear of death appears to have mastered and elaborated a strange and ancient formula by which the grosser factors of the body being eliminated, the more ethereal portions continue to retain the spirit, and the body is thus preserved from absolute disintegration. In this manner true death may be indefinitely deferred. Secure from the ordinary chances and changes of existence, this spiritualised body could retain a modified life practically for ever."

"This is a most extraordinary idea, my dear fellow," remarked Thierry.

"But why should Sir Gilbert haunt the Manor House, and one special room?"

"The tendency of spirits to return to the old haunts of bodily life is almost universal. We cannot yet explain the reason of this attraction of environment."

"But the expansion--the crowding substance which we ourselves felt? You cannot meet that difficulty," said Thierry persistently.

"Not as fully as I could wish, perhaps. But the power of expanding and contracting to a degree far beyond our comprehension is a well-known attribute of spiritualised matter."

"Wait one little moment, my dear Monsieur Flaxman," broke in Thierry's voice after an interval; "this is very clever and ingenious indeed. As a theory I give it my sincere admiration. But proof--proof is what we now demand."

Flaxman Low looked steadily at the two incredulous faces.

"This," he said slowly, "is the hair of Sir Gilbert Blackburton, and this nail is from the little finger of his left hand. You can prove my assertion by opening the coffin."

Sir George, who was pacing up and down the room impatiently, drew up.

"I don't like it at all, Mr. Low, I tell you frankly. I don't like it at all. I see no object in violating the coffin. I am not concerned to verify this unpleasant theory of yours. I have only one desire; I want to get rid of this haunting presence, whatever it is."

"If I am right," replied Low, "the opening of the coffin and exposure of the remains to strong sunshine for a short time will free you for ever from this presence."

In the early morning, when the summer sun struck warmly on the lawns of Yand, the three men carried the coffin from the vault to a quiet spot among the shrubs where, secure from observation, they raised the lid.

Within the coffin lay the semblance of Gilbert Blackburton, maned to the ears with long and coarse black hair. Matted eyelashes swept the fallen cheeks, and beside the body stretched the bony hands, each with its dependent sheaf of switch-like nails. Low bent over and raised the left hand gingerly.

The little finger was without a nail!

Two hours later they came back and looked again. The sun had in the meantime done its work; nothing remained but a fleshless skeleton and a few half-rotten shreds of clothing.

The ghost of Yand Manor House has never since been heard of.

When Thiery bade Flaxman Low good-bye, he said:

"In time, my dear Monsieur Flaxman, you will add another to our sciences. You establish your facts too well for my peace of mind."

The Story of Sevens Hall

"It may be quite true," said Yarkindale gloomily; "all that I can answer is that we always die the same way. Some of us choose, or are driven, to one form of suicide, and some to another, but the result is alike. For three generations every man of my family has died by his own hand. I have not come to you hoping for help, Mr. Low, I merely want to tell the facts to a man who may possibly believe that we are not insane, that heredity and madness have nothing to do with our leaving the world; but that we are forced out of it by some external power acting upon us, I do not know how. If we inherit anything it is clear-headedness and strength of will, but this curse of ours is stronger. That is all."

Flaxman Low kicked the fire into a blaze. It shown on the silver and china of the breakfast service, and on the sallow, despairing face of the man in the arm-chair opposite. He was still young, but already the cloud that rested upon his life had carved deep lines upon his forehead in addition to the long tell-tale groove from mouth to nostril.

"I conclude death does not occur without some premonition. Tell me something more. What precedes death?" inquired Flaxman Low.

"A regular and well-marked series of events--I insist upon calling them events," replied Yarkindale. "This is not a disease with a series of symptoms. Whatever it is it comes from the outside. First we fall into an indescribable depression, causeless except as being the beginning of the end, for we are all healthy men, fairly rich, and even lucky in the other affairs of life--and of love. Next comes the ghost or apparition or whatever you like to call it. Lastly we die by our own hands." Yarkindale brought down a sinewy brown hand upon the arm of his chair. "And because we have been powers in the land, and there must be as little scandal as possible, the doctors and the coroner's jury bring it in 'Temporary insanity.'"

"How long does this depression last before the end?" Flaxman Low's voice broke in upon the other's moody thinking.

"That varies, but the conclusion never. I am the last of the lot, and though I am full of life and health and resolve today, I don't give myself a week to live. It is ghastly! To kill oneself is bad enough, but to know that one is being driven to do it, to know that no power on earth can save us, is an outlook of which words can't give the colour."

"But you have not yet seen the apparition--which is the second stage."

"It will come to-day or to-morrow--as soon as I go back to Sevens Hall. I have watched two others of my family go through the same mill. This irresistible depression always comes first. I tell you, in two weeks I shall be dead. And the thought is maddening me!

"I have a wife and child," he went on after an interval; "and to think of the poor little beggar growing up only to suffer this!"

"Where are they?" asked Low.

"I left them in Florence. I hope the truth can be kept from my wife; but that also is too much to hope. 'Another suicide at Sevens Hall.' I can see the headlines. Those rags of newspapers would sell their mothers for half-a-crown!"

"Then the other deaths took place at Sevens Hall?"

"All of them." He stopped and looked hard at Mr. Low.

"Tell me about your brothers," said Low.

Yarkindale burst into laughter.

"Well done, Mr. Low! Why didn't you advise me not to go back to Sevens Hall? That is the admirable counsel which the two brain specialists, whom I have seen since I came up to town, have given me. Go back to the Hall? Of course I shouldn't--if I could help it. That's the difficulty--I can't help it! I must go. They thought me mad!"

"I hardly wonder," said Low calmly, "if you exhibited the same excitement. Now, hear me. If, as you wish me to suppose, you are fighting against supernatural powers, the very first point is to keep a firm and calm control of your feelings and thoughts. It is possible that you and I together may be able to meet this trouble of yours in some new and possibly successful way. Tell me all you can remember with regard to the deaths of your brothers."

"You are right," said Yarkindale sadly enough. "I am behaving like a maniac, and yet I'm sane, Heaven knows!--To begin with, there were three of us, and we made up our minds long ago when we were kids to see each other through to the last, and we determined not to yield to the influence without a good fight for it. Five years ago my eldest brother went to Somaliland on a shooting trip. He was big, vigorous, self-willed man, and I was not anxious about him. My second brother, Jack, was an R.E., a clever, sensitive, quiet fellow, more likely to be affected by the tradition of the family. While he was out in Gib., Vane suddenly returned from Africa. I found him changed. He had become gloomy and abstracted, and kept saying that the curse was coming up- on him. He insisted upon going down to Sevens Hall. I was savage with him. I thought he should have resisted the inclination; I know more about it now. One night he rushed into my bedroom, crying out: 'He's come; he's come!'"

"Did he ever describe what he had seen?" asked Low.

"Never. None of us know definitely what shape the cursed thing takes. No one of us has ever seen it; or, at any rate, in time to describe it. But once it comes--and this is the horrible part--it never leaves us. Step by step it dogs us, till--" Yarkindale stopped, and in a minute or two resumed. "For two nights I sat up with him. He said very little, for Vane never talked much; but I saw the agony in his face, the fear, the loathing, the growing horror--he, who I believe, had never before feared anything in his life.

"The third night I fell asleep. I was worn out, though I don't offer that as an excuse. I am a light sleeper, yet while I slept Vane killed himself within six feet of me! At the inquest it was proved he had bought a silken waist-rope at Cairo, and it was contended that he must have concealed it from me, as I had never seen it. I found him with his head nearly twisted off, and a red rubbed weal across his face. He was lying in a heap upon the floor, for the rope was frayed and broken by his struggles. The theory was that he had hanged himself, and then repented of it, and in his efforts to get free had wrenched his head around, and scarred his face."

Yarkindale stopped and shuddered violently.

"I tried to hush the matter up as well as I could, but of course the news of it reached Jack. Then a couple of years passed, and he went from Gib. to India, and wrote in splendid spirits, for he had met a girl he liked out there, and he had told me that there was never so happy a man on earth before. So you can fancy how I felt when I had a wire from the Hall imploring me to go down at once for Jack had arrived. It is very hard to tell you what he suffered." Yarkindale broke off and wiped his forehead. "For I have been through it all within the last two weeks myself. He cared for that girl beyond anything on earth; yet within a couple of days of their marriage, he had felt himself impelled to rush home to England without so much as bidding her good-bye, though he knew that at the end of his journey death was waiting for him. We talked it over rationally, Mr. Low, and we determined to combine against the power, whatever it was, that was driving him out of the world. We are not monomaniacs. We want to live; we have all that makes life worth living; and yet I am going the same way, and not any effort or desire or resolution on my part can save me!"

"It is a pity you make up your mind to that," said Flaxman Low. "One will pitted against another will has at least a chance of success. And a second point I beg you will bear in mind. Good is always inherently stronger than evil. If, for instance, health were not, broadly speaking, stronger than disease, the poisonous germs floating about the world would kill off the human race inside twelve months."

"Yes," said Yarkindale; "but where two of us failed before, it is not likely that I alone will succeed."

"You need not be alone," said Flaxman Low; "for if you have no objection, I should be glad to accompany you to Sevens Hall, and to give you any aid that may be in my power."

It is not necessary to record what Yarkindale had to say in answer to this offer. Presently he resumed his story:

"Jack was dispirited, and unlike Vane, desperately afraid of his fate. He hardly dare to fall asleep. He recalled all he knew of our father's death, and tried to draw me on to describe Vane's, but I knew better than that. Still, with all my care, he went the same way! I did not trust my own watchfulness a second time; I had a man in the house who was a trained attendant. He sat outside Jack's door of nights. One morning early--it was summer-time, and he must have dropped into a doze--he was shoved over, chair and all, and before he could pick himself up, Jack had flung himself from the balcony outside one of the gallery windows."

Sevens Hall is a large Elizabethan mansion hidden away among acres of rich pasture lands, where wild flowers bloom abundantly in their seasons and rooks build and caw in the great elms. But none of the natural beauties of the country were visible when Mr. Low arrived late on a November evening with Yarkindale. The interior of the house, however, made up for the bleakness outside. Fires and lights blazed in the hall and in the principal rooms. During dinner, Yarkindale seemed to have relapsed into his most dejected mood. He scarcely opened his lips, and his face looked black, not only with depression, but anger. For he was by no means ready to give up life; he rebelled against his fate with the strenuous fury of a man whose pride and strength of will and nearest desires are baffled by an antagonist he cannot evade.

During the evening they played billiards, for Low was aware that the less his companion thought over his own position, the better.

Flaxman Low arranged to occupy a room opposite Yarkindale's. So far the latter was in the same state as on the day when he first saw Mr. Low. He was conscious of the same deep and causeless depression, and the wish to return to Sevens Hall had grown beyond his power to resist. But the second of the fatal signs, the following footsteps, had not yet been heard.

During the next forenoon, to Yarkindale's surprise, Flaxman Low, instead of avoiding the subject, threshed out the details of the former deaths at Sevens Hall, especially those of which Yarkindale could give the fullest particulars. He examined the balcony from which Jack Yarkindale had thrown himself. The ironwork was wrenched and broken in one part.

"When did this happen?" asked Low, pointing to it.

"On the night that Jack died," was the reply. "I have been very little at home since, and I did not care at the time to bother about having it put right."

"It looks," said Flaxman Low, "as if he had a struggle for his life, and clung to the upper bar here where it is bent outwards. He had wounds on his hands, had he not?" he continued looking at a dull long splash of rust upon the iron.

"Yes, his hands were bleeding."

"Please try to recollect exactly. Were they cut or bruised upon the palm? Or was it on the back?"

"Now I come to think of it, his hands were a good deal injured, especially on the knuckles--one wrist was broken--by the fall no doubt."

Flaxman Low made no remark.

Next they went into the spacious bedroom where Vane and more of one of those who went before him had died, and which Yarkindale now occupied. His companion asked to see the rope with which Vane had hanged himself. Most unwillingly Yarkindale brought it out. The two pieces, with their broken strands and brown stains, appeared to be of great interest to Low. He next saw the exact spot on the great bedstead from which it had been suspended, and searching along the back, he discovered the jagged edge of the wood against which Vane in his last agony had endeavoured to free himself by fraying the rope.

"We suppose the rope gave after he was dead, and that was because of his great weight," said Yarkindale. "This is he room in which most of the tragedies have taken place. You will probably witness the last one."

"That will depend on yourself," answered Flaxman Low. "I am inclined to think there will be no tragedy if you will stiffen your back, and hold out. Did either of your brothers on waking complain of dreams?"

Yarkindale looked suspiciously a him under drawn brows. "Yes," he said harshly, "they both spoke of tormenting dreams, which they could not recall after walking, but that was also taken as a symptom of brain disease by the experts. And now that you have learned about the matter, you, too, begin upon the old, worn theory."

"On the contrary, my theory has nothing to do with insanity, though the phenomena connected with the deaths of your brothers seem to be closely associated with sleep. You tell me that your brother Jack was afraid to sleep. Your other brother awoke to find his death somehow. Therefore, we may be certain that at a certain stage of these series of events, as you call them, sleep becomes both a dread and a danger."

Yarkindale shivered and glanced nervously over his shoulder.

"This room is growing very cold. Let us go down to the hall. As to sleep, I have been afraid of it for a long time."

All the day Low noticed that his companion continued to look excessively pale and nervous. Every now and then he would turn his face round as if listening. In the evening they again played billiards late into the night. The house was full of silence before they went upstairs. A long strip of polished flooring led from the billiard-room door to the hall. Yarkindale motioned to Low to stand still while he walked slowly to the foot of the staircase. In the stillness Flaxman Low distinctly heard mingled steps, a softer tread following upon Yarkindale's purposely loud footfalls. The hall was in darkness with the exception of a gas jet at the staircase. Yarkindale stopped, leant heavily against the pillar of the balustrade, and with a ghastly face waited for Low to join him. Then he gripped Low by the arm and pointed downwards. Beside his shadow, a second dim, hooded, formless shadow showed faintly on the floor.

"Stage two," said Yarkindale, "You can see it is no fancy of our unhealthy brains."

Mr. Low has placed it upon record that the following week contained one of the most painful experiences through which it has been his lot to pass. Yarkindale fought doggedly for his life. He thrust aside his dejection. He followed the advice given him with marvellous courage. But still the ominous days dragged on, seeming at times too slow,

at times too rapid in their passage. Yarkindale's physical strength began to fail--a mental battle is the most exhausting of all struggles.

"The next point in which you can help," said Low on the eighth
night, "is to try to recollect what you have been dreaming of immediately before waking."

Yarkindale shook his head despondently.

"I have tried over and over again, and though I wake in a cold
sweat of terror, I cannot gather my senses quickly enough to seize the
remembrance of the thing that has spoiled my sleep," he answered
with a pallid smile. "You think the psychological moment with us is
undoubtedly the first waking moment?"

Low admitted that he thought it was so.

"I understand now why you have emptied this room of everything
except the two couches on which we lie. You are afraid I shall lay
hands upon myself! I feel the danger and yet I have no suicidal desire.
I want to live--Heaven, how I long to live! To be happy, and prosper-
ous, and light-hearted as I was once was!"

Yarkindale lay back upon the couch.

"I wish I could give you the faintest notion of the desperate misery
in my mind to-night! I could almost ask to die to escape from it!" he
went on; "the burden only appears to grow heavier and more unbeara-
ble every day--I sometimes feel I can no longer endure it."

"Think, on the contrary, how much you have to live for. For your
own self it matters less than for your boy. Your victory may mean
his."

"How? Tell me how?"

"It is rather a long explanation, and I think we had better defer it
until I can form some definite ideas on the subject."

"Very well." Yarkindale turned his face from the light. "I will try to
sleep and forget all this wretchedness if I can. You will not leave me?"

Through the long winter night, Flaxman Low watched beside him.
He felt he dared not leave him for one moment. The room was almost
dark, for Yarkindale could not sleep otherwise. The flickering firelight
died down, until nothing was left of the last layer of glowing wood
ashes. The night lamp in a distant corner threw long shadows across
the empty floor, that wavered now and then as if a wind touched the
flame.

Outside the night was still and black; not a sound disturbed the silence except those strange unaccountable creakings and groanings
which seem like inarticulate voices in an old house.

Yarkindale was sleeping heavily, and as the night deepened Low got up and walked about the room in circles, always keeping his face towards the sleeper. The air had grown very cold, and when he sat down again he drew a rug about him, and lit a cigar. The change in the atmosphere was sudden and peculiar, and he softly pulled his couch close to Yarkindale's and waited.

Creakings and groanings floated up and down the gaunt old corridors, the mystery and loneliness of night became oppressive. The shadow from the night lamp swayed and fluttered as if a door had been opened. Mr. Low glanced at both doors. He had locked both, and both were closed, yet the flame bent and flickered until Low put his hand across his companion's chest, so that he might detect any waking movement, for the light had now become too dim to see by.

To his intense surprise he found his hand at once in the chill of a cold draught blowing on it from above. But Flaxman Low had no time to think about it, for a terrible feeling of cold and numbness was stealing upwards through his feet, and a sense of weighty and deadly chill seemed pressing in upon his shoulders and back. The back of his neck ached, his outstretched hand began to stiffen.

Yarkindale still slept heavily.

New sensations were borne in slowly upon Low. The chill around him was the repulsive clammy chill of a thing long dead. Desperate desires awoke in his mind; something that could almost be felt was beating down his will.

Then Yarkindale moved slightly in his sleep.

Low was conscious of a supreme struggle, whether of mind or body he does not know, but to him it appeared to extend to the ultimate effort a man can make. A hideous temptation rushed wildly across his thoughts to murder Yarkindale! A dreadful longing to feel the man's strong throat yielding and crushing under his own sinewy strangling fingers, was forced into his mind.

Suddenly, Low became aware that, although the couch and part of Yarkindale's figure were visible, his head and the upper part of his body were blotted out as if by some black intervening object. But there was no outline of the interposed form, nothing but a vague thick blackness.

He sprang to his feet as he heard an ominous choking gasp from Yarkindale, and with his swift hands he felt over the body through the darkness. Yarkindale lay tense and stiff.

"Yarkindale!" shouted Low, as his fingers felt the angle of an elbow, then hands upon Yarkindale's throat, hands that clutched savagely with fingers of iron.

"Wake man!" shouted Low again, trying to loosen the desperate clutch. Then he knew that the hands were Yarkindale's hands, and that the man was apparently strangling himself.

The ghastly struggle, that in the darkness, seemed half a dream and half reality, ceased abruptly when Yarkindale moved and his hands fell limp and slack into Low's as the darkness between them cleared away.

"Are you awake?" Low called again.

"Yes. What is it? I feel as if I had been fighting for my life. Or have I been very ill?"

"Both, in a sense. You have passed the crisis, and you are still living. Hold on, the lamp's gone out."

But, as he spoke, the light resumed its steady glimmer, and, when a couple of candles added their brightness, the room was shown bare and empty, and as securely closed as ever. The only change to be noted was that the temperature had risen.

A frosty sun was shining into the library windows next morning when Flaxman Low talked out the matter of the haunting presence which had exerted so sinister an influence upon generations of the Yarkindale family.

"Before you say anything, I wish to admit, Mr. Low, that I, and no doubt those who have gone before me, have certainly suffered from a transient touch of suicidal mania," began Yarkindale gloomily.

"And I am very sure you make a mistake," replied Low. "In suicidal mania the idea is not transient, but persistent, often extending over months, during which time the patient watches for an opportunity to make away with himself. In your case, when I woke you last night, you were aware of a desire to strangle yourself, but directly you became thoroughly awake, the idea left you?"

"That is so. Still--"

"You know that often when dreaming one imagines oneself to do many things which in the waking state would be entirely impossible, yet one continues subject to the idea for a moment or so during the intermittent stage between waking and sleeping. If one has a nightmare, one continues to feel a beating of the heart and a sensation of fright even for some interval after waking. Yours was an analogous condition."

"But look here, Mr. Low. How do you account for it that I, who at this moment have not the slightest desire to make away with myself, should, at the moment of awaking from sleep, be driven to doing that which I detest and wish to avoid?"

"In every particular," said Flaxman Low, "your brothers' cases were similar. Each of them attempted his life in that transient moment while the will and reason were still passive, and action was still subject to an abnormally vivid idea which had evidently been impressed upon the consciousness during sleep. We have clear proof of this, I say, in the struggles of each to save himself when actually in extremis. Contemporary psychology has arrived at the conclusion that every man possesses a subconscious as well as a conscious self," added Low, after a pause. "This second or submerged self appears to be infinitely more susceptible of spiritual influences than the conscious personality. Such influences work most strongly when the normal self is in abeyance during sleep, dreaming, or the hypnotic condition. In your own family you have an excellent example of the idea of self-destruction being suggested during sleep, and carried into action during the first confused, unmastered moments of waking."

"But how do you account for the following footsteps? Whose wishes or suggestions do we obey?"

"I believe them to be different manifestations of the same evil intelligence. Ghosts sometimes, as possibly you are aware, pursue a purpose, and your family has been held in subjection by a malicious spirit that has goaded them on to destroy themselves. I could bring forward a number of other examples; there is the Black Friar of the Sinclairs and the Fox of the Oxenholms. To come back to your own case--do you remember of what you dreamed before I woke you?"

Yarkindale looked troubled.

"I have a dim recollection, but it eludes me. I cannot fix it." He glanced round the room, as if searching for a reminder. Suddenly he sprang up and approached a picture on the wall--"Here it is!" he shouted. "I remember now. A dark figure stood over me; I saw the long face and the sinister eyes--Jules Cevaine!"

"You have not spoken of Cevaine before. Who was he?"

"He was the last of the old Cevaines. You know this house is called Sevens Hall--a popular corruption of the Norman name Cevaine. We Yarkindales were distant cousins, and inherited this place after the death of Jules Cevain, about a hundred years ago. He was said to have taken a prominent part--under another name--in the Reign of Terror. However that may be--he resented our inheriting the Hall."

"He died here?" asked Flaxman Low.

"Yes."

"His purpose in haunting you," said Low, "was doubtless the extermination of your family. His spirit lingers about this spot where the final intense passion of terror, pain, and hatred was felt. And you yourselves have unknowingly fostered his power by dwelling upon and dreading his influence, thus opening the way to spirit communication, until from time to time his disembodied will has superimposed itself upon your wills during the bewildered moment of waking, and the several successive tragedies of which you told me have been the result."

"Then how can we ever escape?"

"You have already won one and your most important victory; for the rest, think of him as seldom as may be. Destroy this painting and any other articles that may have belonged to him; and if you take my advice you will travel for a while."

In pursuance of Mr. Flaxman Low's advice, Yarkindale went for the cold weather to India. He has had no recurrence of the old trouble, but he loathes Sevens Hall, and he is only waiting for his son to be old enough to break the entail, when the property will be placed on the market.

The Story of Saddler's Croft

Although Flaxman Low has devoted his life to the study of psychical phenomena, he has always been most earnest in warning persons who feel inclined to dabble in spiritualism, without any serious motive for doing so, of the mischief and danger accruing to the rash experimenter.

Extremely few persons are sufficiently masters of themselves to permit of their calling in the vast unknown forces outside ordinary human knowledge for mere purposes of amusement.

In support of this warning the following extraordinary story is laid before our readers.

Deep in the forest land of Sussex, close by an unfrequented road, stands a low half-timbered house, that is only separated from the roadway by a rough stone wall and a few flower borders.

The front is covered with ivy, and looks out between two conical trees upon the passers-by. The windows are many of them diamond-paned, and an unpretentious white gate leads up to the front door. It is a quaint, quiet spot, with an old-world suggestion about it which appealed strongly to pretty Sadie Corcoran as she drove with her husband along the lane. The Corcorans were Americans, and had to the full the American liking for things ancient. Saddler's Croft struck them both as ideal, and when they found out that it was much more roomy and comfortable than it looked from the road, and also that it had large lawns and grounds attached to it, they decided at once on taking it for a year or two.

When they mentioned the project to Phil Strewd, their host, and an old friend of Corcoran, he did not favour it. Much as he should have liked to have them for neighbours, he thought that Saddler's Croft had too many unpleasant traditions connected with it. Besides, it had lain empty for three years, as the last occupants were spiritualists of some sort, and the place was said to be haunted. But Mrs. Corcoran was not to be put off, and declared that a flavour of ghostliness was all that Saddler's Croft required to make it absolutely the most attractive residence in Europe.

The Corcorans moved in about October, but it was not till the following July that Flaxman Low met Mr. Strewd on the Victoria platform.

"I'm glad you're coming down to Andy Corcoran's," Strewd began. "You must remember him? I introduced you to him at the club a couple of years ago. He's an awfully decent fellow, and an old friend of mine. He once went with an Arctic expedition, and has crossed Greenland or San Josef's Land on snowshoes or something. I've got the book about it at home. So you can size him up for yourself. He's now married to a very pretty woman, and they have taken a house in my part of the world.

"I didn't want them to rent Saddler's Croft, for it had a bad name some years ago. Some of your psychical folk used to live there. They made a sort of Greek temple at the back, where they used to have queer goings on, so I'm told. A Greek was living with them called Agapoulos, who was the arch-priest of their sect, or whatever it was. Ultimately Agapoulos died on a moonlight night in the temple, in the middle of their rites. After that his friends left, but, of course, people said he haunted the place. I never saw anything myself, but a young sailor, home on leave about that time, swore he'd catch the ghost, and he was found next morning on the temple steps. He was past telling us what had happened, or what he had seen, for he was dead. I'll never forget his face. It was horrible!"

"And since then?"

"After that the place would not let, although the talk of the ghost being seen died away until quite lately. I suppose the old caretaker went to bed early, and avoided trouble that way. But during the last few months Corcoran has seen it repeatedly himself, and--in fact, things seem to be going on very strangely. What with Mrs. Corcoran wild on studying psychology, as she calls it--"

"So Mrs. Corcoran has a turn that way?"

"Yes, since young Sinclair came home from Ceylon about five months ago. I must tell you he was very thick with Agapoulos in former times, and people said he used to join in all the ruffianism at Saddler's Croft. You'll see the rest for yourself. You are asked down ostensibly to please Mrs. Corcoran, but Andy hopes you may help him to clear up the mystery."

Flaxman Low found Corcoran a tall, thin, nervy American of the best type; while his wife was as pretty and as charming as we have grown accustomed to expect an American girl to be.

"I suppose," Corcoran began, "that Phil has been giving you all the gossip about this house? I was entirely sceptical once; but now--do you believe in midsummer madness?"

"I believe there often is a deep truth hidden in common beliefs and superstitions. But let me hear more."

"I'll tell you what happened not twenty-four hours ago. Everything has been working up to it for the last three months, but it came to a head last night, and I immediately wired for you. I had been sitting in my smoking-room rather late reading. I put out the lamp and was just about to go to bed when the brilliance of the moonlight struck me, and I put my head through the window to look over the lawn. Directly I heard chanting of a most unusual character from the direction of the temple, which lies at the back of that plantation. Then one voice, a beautiful tenor, detached itself from the rest, and seemed to approach the house. As it came nearer I saw my wife cross the grass to the plantation with a wavering, uncertain gait. I ran after her, for I believed she was walking in her sleep; but before I could reach her a man came out of the grass alley at the other side of the lawn.

"I saw them go away together down the alley towards the temple, but I could not stir, the moonbeams seemed to be penetrating my brain, my feet were chained, the wildest and most hideous thoughts seemed rocking--I can use no other term--in my head. I made an effort, and ran round by another way, and met them on the temple steps. I had strength left to grasp at the man--remember I saw him plainly, with his dark, Greek face--but he turned aside and leapt into the underwood, leaving in my hand only the button from the back of his coat.

"Now comes the incomprehensible part. Sadie, without seeing me, or so it appeared, glided away again towards the house; but I was determined to find the man who had eluded me. The moonlight poured upon my head; I felt it like an absolute touch. The chanting grew louder, and drowned every other recollection. I forgot Sadie, I forgot all but the delicious sounds, and I--I, a nineteenth-century, hard-headed Yankee--hammered at those accursed doors to be allowed to enter. Then, like a dream, the singing was behind me and around me--some one came, or so I thought, and pushed me gently in. The moon was pouring through the end window; there were many people. In the morning I found myself lying on the floor of the temple, and all about me the dust was undisturbed but for the mark of my own single footstep and the spot where I had fallen. You may say it was all a dream, Low, but I tell you some infernal power hangs about that building."

"From what you tell me," said Flaxman Low, "I can almost undertake to say that Mrs. Corcoran is at present nearly, if not quite, ignorant of the horrible experience you remember. In her case the emotions of wonder and curiosity have probably alone been worked upon as in a dream."

"I believe in her absolutely," exclaimed Corcoran, "but this power swamps all resistance. I have another strange circumstance to add. On coming to myself I found the button still in my hand. I have since had the opportunity of fitting it to its right position in the coat of a man who is a pretty constant visitor here," the American's lips tightened, "a young Sinclair, who does tea-planting in Ceylon when he has the health for it, but is just now at home to recruit. He is the son of a neighbouring squire, and in every particular of face and figure unlike the handsome Greek I saw that night."

"Have you spoken to him on the subject?"

"Yes; I showed him the button, and told him I had found it near the temple. He took the news very curiously. He did not look confused or guilty, but simply scared out of his senses. He offered no explanation, but made a hasty excuse, and left us. My wife looked on with the most perfect indifference, and offered no remark."

"Has Mrs. Corcoran appeared to be very languid of late?" asked Low.

"Yes, I have noticed that."

"Judging from the effect produced by the chanting upon you, I should say that you were something of a musician?" said Low irrelevantly.

"Yes," replied the other, astonished.

"Then, this evening, when I am talking with Mrs. Corcoran, will you reproduce the melody you heard on that night?"

Corcoran agreed, and the conversation ended with a request on the part of Mr. Low to be permitted to make the acquaintance of Mrs. Corcoran, and further, to be given the opportunity of talking to her alone.

Sadie Corcoran received him with effusion.

"O Mr. Low, I'm just perfectly delighted to see you! I'm looking forward to the most lovely spiritual talks. It's such fun! You know I was in quite a psychical set before I married, but afterwards I dropped it, because Andy has some effete old prejudices."

Flaxman Low inquired how it happened that her interest had revived.

"It is the air of this dear old place," she replied, with a more serious expression. "I always found the subject very attractive, and lately we have made the acquaintance of a Mr. Sinclair, who is a--" she checked herself with an odd look, "who knows all about it."

"How does he advise you to experiment?" asked Mr. Low. "Have you ever tried sleeping with the moonlight on your face?"

She flushed, and looked startled.

"Yes, Mr. Sinclair told me that the spiritualists who formerly lived in this house believed that by doing so you could put yourself into communication with--other intelligences. It makes one dream," she added, "such strange dreams."

"Are they pleasant dreams?" asked Flaxman Low gravely.

"Not now, but by and by he assures me that they will be."

"But you must think of your dreams all day long, or the moonlight will not affect you so readily on the next occasion, and you are obliged to repeat a certain formula? Is it not so?"

She admitted it was, and added: "But Mr. Sinclair says that if I persevere I shall soon pass through the zone of the bad spirits and enter the circle of the good. So I choose to go on. It is all so wonderful and exciting. Oh, here is Mr. Sinclair! I'm sure you will find many interesting things to talk over.". The drawing-room lay at the back of the house, and overlooked a strip of lawn shut in on the further side by a thick plantation of larches. Directly opposite to the French window, where they were seated, a grass alley which had been cut through the plantation gave a glimpse of turf and forest land beyond. From this alley now emerged a young man in riding-breeches, who walked moodily across the lawn with his eyes on the ground. In a few minutes Flaxman Low understood that young Sinclair had a pronounced admiration for his hostess, the reckless, headstrong admiration with which a weak-willed man of strong emotions often deceives himself and the woman he loves. He was manifestly in wretched health and equally wretched spirits, a combination that greatly impaired the very ordinary type of English good-looks which he represented.

While the three had tea together Mrs. Corcoran made some attempt to lead up to the subject of spiritualism, but Sinclair avoided it, and soon Mrs. Corcoran lost her vivacity, which gave place to a well-marked languor, a condition that Low shortly grew to connect with Sinclair's presence.

Presently she left them, and the two men went outside and walked up and down smoking for a while till Flaxman Low turned down the path between the larches. Sinclair hung back.

"You'll find it stuffy down there," he said, with curved nostrils.

"I rather wanted to see what building that roof over the trees belongs to," replied Low.

With manifest reluctance Sinclair went on beside him. Another turn at right angles brought them into the path leading up to the little temple, which Low found was solidly built of stone. In shape it was oblong, with a pillared Ionic façade. The trees stood closely round it, and it contained only one window, now void of glass, set high in the further end of the building. Low asked a question.

"It was a summer-house made by the people who lived here formerly," replied Sinclair, with brusqueness. "Let's get away. It's beastly damp."

"It is an odd kind of summer-house. It looks more like--" Low checked himself. "Can we go inside?" He went up the low steps and tried the door, which yielded readily, and he entered to look round.

The walls had once been ornamented with designs in black and some glittering pigment, while at the upper end a dais nearly four feet high stood under the arched window, the whole giving the vague impression of a church. One or two peculiarities of structure and decoration struck Low.

He turned sharply on Sinclair.

"What was this place used for?"

But Sinclair was staring round with a white, working face; his glance seemed to trace out the half-obliterated devices upon the walls, and then rested on the dais. A sort of convulsion passed over his features, as his head was jerked forward, rather as if pushed by some unseen force than by his own will, while, at the same time, he brought his hand to his mouth, and kissed it. Then with a strange, prolonged cry he rushed headlong out of the temple, and appeared no more at Saddler's Croft that day.

The afternoon was still and warm with brooding thunderstorm, but at night the sky cleared.

Now it happened that Andy Corcoran was, amongst many other good things, an accomplished musician, and, while Flaxman Low and Mrs. Corcoran talked at intervals by the open French window, he sat down at the piano and played a weird melody. Mrs. Corcoran broke off in the middle of a sentence, and soon she began swaying gently to the rhythm of the music, and presently she was singing. Suddenly,

Corcoran dropped his hand on the notes with a crash. His wife sprang from her chair.

"Andy! Where are you? Where are you?" And in a moment she had thrown herself, sobbing hysterically, into his arms, while he begged her to tell him what troubled her.

"It was that music. Oh, don't play it any more! I liked it at first, and then all at once it seemed to terrify me!" He led her back towards the light.

"Where did you learn that song, Sadie? Tell me."

She lifted her clear eyes to his.

"I don't know! I can't remember, but it is like a dreadful memory! Never play it again! Promise me!"

"Of course not, darling."

By midnight the moon sailed broad and bright above the house. Flaxman Low and the American were together in the smoking-room. The room was in darkness. Low sat in the shadow of the open window, while Corcoran waited behind him in the gloom. The shade of the larches lay in a black line along the grass, the air was still and heavy, not a leaf moved. From his position, Low could see the dark masses of the forest stretching away into the dimness over the undulating country. The scene was very lovely, very lonely, and very sad.

A little trill of bells within the room rang the half-hour after midnight, and scarcely had the sound ceased when from outside came another--a long cadenced wailing chant of voices in unison that rose and fell faint and far off but with one distinct note, the same that Low had heard in Sinclair's beast-like cry earlier in the day.

After the chanting died away, there followed a long sullen interval, broken at last by a sound of singing, but so vague and dim that it might have been some elusive air throbbing within the brain. Slowly it grew louder and nearer. It was the melody Sadie had begged never to hear again, and it was sung by a tenor voice, vibrating and beautiful.

Low felt Corcoran's hand grip his shoulder, when out upon the grass Sadie, a slim figure in trailing white, appeared advancing with uncertain steps towards the alley of the larches. The next moment the singer came forward from the shadows to meet her. It was not Sinclair, but a much more remarkable-looking personage. He stopped and raised his face to the moon, a face of an extraordinary perfection of beauty such as Flaxman Low had never seen before. But the great dark eyes, the full powerfully moulded features, had one attribute in common with Sinclair's face, they wore the same look of a profound and infinite unhappiness.

"Come." Corcoran gripped Flaxman Low's shoulder. "She is sleep-walking. We will see who it is this time."

When they reached the lawn the couple had disappeared. Corcoran leading, the two men ran along under the shadow of the house, and so by another path to the back of the temple.

The empty window glowed in the light of the moon, and the hum of a subdued chanting floated out amongst the silent trees. The sound seized upon the brain like a whiff of opium, and a thousand unbidden thoughts ran through Flaxman Low's mind. But his mental condition was as much under his control as his bodily movements. Pulling himself together he ran on. Sadie Corcoran and her companion were mounting the steps under the pillars. The girl held back, as if drawn forward against her will; her eyes were blank and open, and she moved slowly.

Then Corcoran dashed out of the shadow.

What occurred next Mr. Low does not know, for he hurried Mrs. Corcoran away towards the house, holding her arm gently. She yielded to his touch, and went silently beside him to the drawing-room, where he guided her to a couch. She lay down upon it like a tired child, and closed her eyes without a word.

After a while Flaxman Low went out again to look for Corcoran. The temple was dark and silent, and there was no one to be seen. He groped his way through the long grass towards the back of the building. He had not gone far when he stumbled over something soft that moved and groaned. Low lit a match, for it was impossible to see anything in the gloom under the trees. To his horror he found the American at his feet, beaten and battered almost beyond recognition.

The first thing next morning Mr. Strewd received a note from Flaxman Low asking him to come over at once. He arrived in the course of the forenoon, and listened to an account of Corcoran's adventures during the night, with an air of dismay.

"So it's come at last!" he remarked, "I'd no idea Sinclair was such a bruiser."

"Sinclair? What do you suppose Sinclair had to do with it?"

"Oh, come now, Low, what's the good of that? Why, my man told me this morning when I was shaving that Sinclair went home some time last night all covered in blood. I'd half a guess at what had happened then."

"But I tell you I saw the man with whom Corcoran fought. He was an extraordinarily handsome man with a Greek face."

Strewd whistled.

"By George, Low, you let your imagination run away with you," he said, shaking his head.

"That's all nonsense, you know."

"We must try to find out if it is," said Low.

"Will you come over to-night and stay with me? There will be a full moon."

"Yes, and it has affected all your brains! Here's Mrs. Corcoran full of surprise over her husband's condition! You don't suppose that's genuine?"

"I know it is genuine," replied Low quietly. "Bring your Kodak with you when you come, will you?"

The day was long, languorous, and heavy; the thunderstorm had not yet broken, but once again the night rose cloudless. Flaxman Low decided to watch alone near the temple while Strewd remained on the alert in the house, ready to give his help if it should be needed.

The hush of the night, the smell of the dewy larches, the silvery light with its bewildering beauty creeping from point to point as the moon rose, all the pure influences of nature, seemed to Low more powerful, more effective, than he had ever before felt them to be. Forcing his mind to dwell on ordinary subjects, he waited. Midnight passed, and then began indistinct sounds, shuffling footsteps, murmurings, and laughter, but all faint and evasive. Gradually the tumultuous thoughts he had experienced on the previous evening began to run riot in his brain.

When the singing began he does not know. It was only by an immense effort of will that he was able to throw off the trance that was stealing over him, holding him prisoner--how nearly a willing prisoner he shudders to remember. But habits of self-control have been Low's only shield in many a dangerous hour. They came to his aid now. He moved out in front of the temple just in time to see Sadie pass within the temple door. Waiting only a moment to make quite sure of his senses, and concentrating his will on the single desire of saving her, he followed. He says he was conscious of a crowd of persons at either side; he knew without looking that the pictures on the wall glowed and lived again.

Through the high window opposite him a broad white shaft of light fell, and immediately under it, on the dais, stood the man whom Mr. Low in his heart now called Agapoulos. Supreme in its beauty and its sadness that beautiful face looked across the bowed heads of those present into the eyes of Mr. Flaxman Low. Slowly, very slowly, as a narrow lane opened up before him amongst the figures of the crowd,

Low advanced towards the daïs. The man's smile seemed to draw him on; he stretched out his hand as Flaxman Low approached. And Low was conscious of a longing to clasp it even though that might mean perdition.

At the last moment, when it seemed to him he could resist no longer, he became aware of the white-clad figure of Sadie beside him. She also was looking up at the beautiful face with a wild gaze. Low hesitated no longer. He was now within two feet of the dais. He swung back his left hand and dealt a smashing half-arm blow at the figure. The man staggered with a very human groan, and then fell face forward on the dais. A whirlwind of dust seemed to rise and obscure the moonlight; there was a wild sense of motion and flight, a subdued sibilant murmur like the noise of a swarm of bats in commotion, and then Flaxman Low heard Phil Strewd's loud voice at the door, and he shouted to him to come.

"What has happened?" said Strewd, as he helped to raise the fallen man. "Why, whom have we got here? Good heavens, Low, it is Agapoulos! I remember him well!"

"Leave him there in the moonlight. Take Mrs. Corcoran away and hurry back with the Kodak. There is no time to lose before the moon leaves this window."

The moonlight was full and strong, the exposure prolonged and steady, so that when afterwards Flaxman Low came to develop the film--but we are anticipating, for the night and its revelations were not over yet. The two men waited through the dark hour that precedes the dawn, intending when daylight came to remove their prisoner elsewhere. They sat on the edge of the daïs side by side, Strewd at Low's request holding the hand of the unconscious man, and talked till the light came.

"I think it's about time to move him now," suggested Strewd, looking round at the wounded man behind him. As he did so, he sprang to his feet with a shout.

"What's this, Low? I've gone mad, I think! Look here!"

Flaxman Low bent over the pale, unconscious face. It bore no longer the impress of that exquisite Greek beauty they had seen an hour earlier; it only showed to their astonished gaze the haggard outlines of young Sinclair.

Some days later Strewd rubbed the back of his head energetically with a broad hand, and surmised aloud.

"This is a strange world, my masters," and he looked across the cool shady bedroom at Andy Corcoran's bandaged head.

"And the other world's stranger, I guess," put in the American drily, "if we may judge by the sample of the supernatural we have lately had.

"You know I hold that there is no such thing as the supernatural; all is natural," said Flaxman Low. "We need more light, more knowledge. As there is a well-defined break in the notes of the human voice, so there is a break between what we call natural and supernatural. But the notes of the upper register correspond with those in the lower scale; in like manner, by drawing upon our experience of things we know and see, we should be able to form accurate hypotheses with regard to things which, while clearly pertaining to us, have so far been regarded as mysteries."

"I doubt if any theory will touch this mystery," Strewd objected. "I have questioned Sinclair, and noted down his answers as you asked me, Low. Here they are."

"No, thank you. Will you compare my theory with what he has told you? In the first place, Agapoulos was, I fancy, one of a clique calling themselves Dianists, who desired to revive the ancient worship of the moon. That I easily gathered from the symbol of the moon in front of the temple and from the half-defaced devices on the walls inside. Then I perceived that Sinclair, when we were standing before the dais, almost unconsciously used the gesture of the moon worshippers. The chant we heard was the lament for Adonis. I could multiply evidences, but there is no need to do so. The fact also tells that the place is haunted on moonlight nights only."

"Sinclair's confession corroborates all this," said Strewd at this point.

Corcoran turned irritably on his couch.

"Moon-worship was not exactly the nicest form of idolatry," he said in a weary tone; "but I can't see how that accounts for the awkward fact that a man who not only looks like Agapoulos, but was caught, and even photographed as Agapoulos, turns out at the end of an hour or so, during which there was no chance of substituting one for the other, to be another person of an entirely different appearance. Add to this that Agapoulos is dead and Sinclair is living, and we have an array of facts that drive one to suspect that common-sense and reason are delusions. Go on, Low."

"The substitution, as you call it, of Agapoulos for Sinclair is one of the most marked and best attested cases of obsession with which I have personally come into contact," answered Flaxman Low. "You will notice that during Sinclair's absence in Ceylon nothing was seen of the ghost---on his return it again appeared."

"What is obsession? I know what it is supposed to be, but--" Corcoran stopped.

"I should call it in this case as nearly as possible an instance of spiritual hypnotism. We know there is such a thing as human hypnotism; why should not a disembodied spirit have similar powers? Sinclair has been obsessed by the spirit of Agapoulos; he not only yielded to his influence in the man's lifetime, but sought it again after his death. I don't profess to claim any great knowledge of the subject, but I do know that terrible results have come about from similar practices. Sinclair, for his own reasons, invited the control of a spirit, and, having no inherent powers of resistance, he became its slave. Agapoulos must have possessed extraordinary will-force; his soul actually dominated Sinclair's. Thus not only the mental attributes of Sinclair but even his bodily appearance became modified to the likeness of the Greek. Sinclair himself probably looked upon his experiences as a series of vivid dreams induced by dwelling on certain thoughts and using certain formulae, until this morning when his condition proved to him that they were real enough."

"That is perhaps all very well so far as it goes," put in Strewd, "but I fail to understand how a seedy, weakly chap like Sinclair could punish my friend Andy here, as we must suppose he has done, if we accept your ideas, Low."

"You are aware that under abnormal conditions, such as may be observed in the insane, a quite extraordinary reserve of latent strength is frequently called out from apparently weak persons. So Sinclair's usual powers were largely reinforced by abnormal influences."

"I have another question to ask, Low," said Corcoran. "Can you explain the strange attraction and influence the temple possessed over all of us, and especially over my wife?"

"I think so. Mrs. Corcoran, through a desire for amusement and excitement, placed herself in a degree of communication with the spiritual world during sleep. Remember, the Greek lived here, and the thoughts and emotions of individuals remain in the aura of places closely associated with them. Personally, I do not doubt that Agapoulos is a strong and living intelligence, and those persons who frequent the vicinity of the temple are readily placed in rapport with his wandering spirit by means of this aura. To use common words, evil influences haunt the temple."

"But this is intolerable. What can we do?"

"Leave Saddler's Croft, and persuade Mrs. Corcoran to have no more to do with spiritism. As for Sinclair, I will see him. He has opened what may be called the doors of life. It will be a hard task to close them again, and to become his own master. But it may be done."

The Story of Konnor Old House

"I HOLD," Mr. Flaxman Low, the eminent psychologist, was saying, "that there are no other laws in what we term the realm of the supernatural but those which are the projections or extensions of natural laws."

"Very likely that's so," returned Naripse, with suspicious humility. "But, all the same, Konnor Old House presents problems that won't work in with any natural laws I'm acquainted with. I almost hesitate to give voice to them, they sound so impossible and--and absurd."

"Let's judge of them," said Low.

"It is said," said Naripse, standing up with his back to the fire, "it is said that a Shining Man haunts the place. Also a light is frequently seen in the library--I've watched it myself of a night from here--yet the dust there, which happens to lie very thick over the floor and the furniture, has afterwards shown no sign of disturbance."

"Have you satisfactory evidence of the presence of the Shining Man?"

"I think so," replied Naripse shortly. "I saw him myself the night before I wrote asking you to come up to see me. I went into the house after dusk, and was on the stairs when I saw him: the tall figure of a man, absolutely white and shining. His back was towards me, but the sullen, raised shoulders and sidelong head expressed a degree of sinister animosity that exceeded anything I've ever met with. So I left him in possession, for it's a fact that anyone who has tried to leave his card at Konnor Old House has left his wits with it."

"It certainly sounds rather absurd," said Mr. Low, "but I suppose we have not heard all about it yet?"

"No, there is a tragedy connected with the house, but it's quite a commonplace sort of story and in no way accounts for the Shining Man."

Naripse was a young man of means, who spent most of his time abroad, but the above conversation took place at the spot to which he always referred as home--a shooting-lodge connected with his big grouse-moor on the West Coast of Scotland. The lodge was a small new house built in a damp valley, with a trout-stream running just beyond the garden-hedge.

From the high ground above, where the moor stretched out towards the Solway Firth, it was possible on a fine day to see the dark cone of Ailsa Crag rising above the shimmering ripples. But Mr. Low happened to arrive in a spell of bad weather, when nothing was visible about the lodge but a few roods of sodden lowland, and a curve of the yellow tumbling little river, and beyond a mirky outline of shouldering hills blurred by the ever-falling rain. It may have been eleven o'clock on a depressing, muggy night, when Naripse began to talk about Konnor Old House as he sat with his guests over a crackling flaming fire of pinewood.

"Konnor Old House stands on a spur of the ridge opposite-one of the finest sites possible, and it belongs to me. Yet I am obliged to live in this damp little boghole, for the man who would pass a night in Konnor is not to be met with in this county!"

Sullivan, the third man present, replied he was, perhaps--with a glance at Low--there were two, which stung Naripse, who turned his words into a deliberate challenge.

"Is it a bet?" asked Sullivan, rising. He was a tallish man, dark, and clean-shaven, whose features were well-known to the public in connection with the emerald green jersey of the Rugby International Football Team of Ireland. "If it is, it's a bet I'm going to win I Goodnight. In the morning, Naripse, I'll trouble you for the difference."

"The affair is much more in Low's line than in yours," said Naripse. "But you're not really going?"

"You may take it I am though!"

"Don't be a fool, Jack! Low, tell him not to go, tell him there are things no man ought to meddle with---" he broke off.

"There are things no man can meddle with," replied Sullivan, obstinately fixing his cap on his head, "and my backing out of this bet would stand in as one of them!"

Naripse was strangely urgent.

"Low, speak to him! You know---"

Flaxman Low saw that the big Irishman's one vanity had got upon its legs; he also saw that Naripse was very much in earnest.

"Sullivan's big enough to take care of himself:" he said laughing. "At the same time, if he doesn't object, we might as well hear the story before he starts."

Sullivan hesitated, then flung his cap into a corner.

"That's so," he said.

It was a warm night for the time of the year, and they could hear, through the open window, the splashing downpour of the rain.

"There's nothing so lonely as the drip of heavy rain!" began Naripse, "I always associate it with Konnor Old House. The place has stood empty for ten years or more, and this is the story they tell about it. It was last inhabited by a Sir James Mackian, who had been a merchant of sorts in Sierra Leone. When the baronetcy fell to him, he came to England and settled down in this place with a pretty daughter and a lot of servants, including a nigger, named Jake, whose life he was said to have saved in Africa. Everything went on well for nearly two years, when Sir James had occasion to go to Edinburgh for a few days. During his absence his daughter was found dead in her bed, having taken an overdose of some sleeping draught. The shock proved too great for her father. He tried travelling, but, on his return home, he fell into a settled melancholy, and died some months later a dumb imbecile at the asylum."

"Well, I shan't object to meeting the girl as she's so pretty," remarked Sullivan with a laugh. "But there's not much in the story."

"Of course," added Naripse, "countryside gossip adds a good deal of colour to the plain facts of the case. It is said that terrible details connected with Miss Mackian's death were suppressed at the inquest, and people recollected afterwards that for months the girl had worn an unhappy, frightened look. It seemed she disliked the negro, and had been heard to beg her father to send him away, but the old man would not listen to her."

"What became of the negro in the end?" asked Flaxman Low.

"In the end Sir James kicked him out after a violent scene, in the course of which he appears to have accused Jake of having some hand in causing the girl's death. The nigger swore he'd be revenged on him, but, as a matter of fact, he left the place almost immediately, and has never been heard of since--which disposes of the nigger. A short time after the old man went mad; he was found lying on a couch in the library--a hopeless imbecile." Saying this, Naripse went to the window, and looked out into the rainy darkness. "Konnor Old House stands on the ridge opposite, and a part of the building, including the library window, where the light is sometimes seen, is visible through the trees from here. There is no light there tonight, though."

Sullivan laughed his big, full laugh.

"How about your shining man? I hope we may have the luck to meet. I suspect some canny Scots tramp knows where to get a snug roost rent free."

"That may be so," replied Naripse, with a slow patience. "I can only say that after seeing the light of a night, I have more than once gone up in the morning to have a look at the library, and never found the thick dust in the least disturbed."

"Have you noticed if the light appears at regular intervals?" said Low.

"No; it's there on and off. I generally see it in rainy weather."

"What sort of people have gone crazy in Konnor Old House?" asked Sullivan.

"One was a tramp. He must have lived pleasantly in the kitchen for days. Then he took to the library, which didn't agree with him apparently. He was found in a dying state lying upon Sir James's couch, with horrible black patches on his face. He was too far gone to speak, so nothing was gleaned from him."

"He probably had a dirty face, and, having caught cold in the rain, went into Konnor Old House and died quietly there of pneumonia or something of the kind, just as you or I might have done, tucked up in our own little beds at home," commented Sullivan.

"The last man to try his luck with the ghosts," went on Naripse, without noticing this remark, "was a young fellow, called Bowie, a nephew of Sir James. He was a student at Edinburgh University and he wanted to clear up the mystery. I was not at home, but my factor allowed him to pass a night in the house. As he did not appear next day, they went to look for him. He was found lying on the couch--and he has not spoken a rational word since."

"Sheer--mere physical fright, acting on an overwrought brain!" Sullivan summed up the case scornfully. "And now I'm off. The rain has stopped, and I'll get up to the house before midnight. You may expect me at dawn to tell you what I've seen."

"What do you intend to do when you get there?" asked Flaxman Low.

"I'll pass the night on the ghostly couch which I suppose I shall find in the library. Take my word for it, madness is in Sir James's family; father and daughter and nephew all gave proof of it in different ways. The tramp, who was perhaps in there for a couple of days, died a natural death. It only needs a healthy man to run the gauntlet and set all this foolish talk at rest."

Naripse was plainly much disturbed though he made no further objection, but when Sullivan was gone, he moved restlessly about the room looking out of the window from time to time. Suddenly he spoke:

"There it is! The light I mentioned to you."

Mr. Low went to the window. Away on the opposite ridge a faint light glimmered out through the thick gloom. Then he glanced at his watch.

"Rather over an hour since he started," he remarked. "Well, now, Naripse, if you will be so good as to hand me 'Human Origins' from the shelf behind you, I think we may settle down to wait for dawn. Sullivan's just the man to give a good account of himself--under most circumstances."

"Heaven send there may be no black side to this business!" said Naripse. "Of course I was a fool to say what I did about the Old House, but nobody except an ass like Jack would think I meant it. I wish the night was well over! That light is due to go out in two hours anyway."

Even to Mr. Low the night seemed unbearably long; but at the first streak of dawn he tossed his book on to the sofa, stretched himself, and said: "We may as well be moving; let's go and see what Sullivan is doing."

The rain began to fall again, and was coming down in close straight lines as the two men drove up the avenue to Konnor Old House. As they ascended, the trees grew thicker on the banks of the cutting which led them in curves to the terrace on which stood the house. Although it was a modern red-brick building, rather picturesque with its gables and sharply-pitched overhanging roofs, it looked desolate and forbidding enough in the grey daybreak. To the left lay lawns and gardens, to the right the cliff fell away steeply to where the burn roared in spate some three hundred feet below. They drove round to the empty stables, and then hurried back to the house on foot by a path that debouched directly under the library window. Naripse stopped under it, and shouted: "Hullo! Jack, where are you?"

But no answer came, and they went on to the hall door. The gloom of the wet dawning and the heavy smell of stagnant air filled the big hall as they looked round at its dreary emptiness. The silence within the house itself was oppressive. Again Naripse shouted, and the noise echoed harshly through the passages, jarring on the stillness, then he led the way to the library at a run.

As they came in sight of the doorway a wave of some nauseating odour met them, and at the same moment they saw Sullivan lying just outside the threshold, his body twisted and rigid like a man in the extremity of pain, his contorted profile ivory-pale against the dark oak flooring, As they stooped to raise him, Mr. Low had just time to notice the big gloomy room beyond, with its heaped and trampled layers of accumulated dust. There was no time for more than a glance, for the indescribable, fetid odour almost overpowered them as they hastened to carry Sullivan into the open air.

"We must get him home as soon as we can," said Mr. Low, "for we have a very sick man on our hands."

This proved to be true. But in a few days, thanks to Mr. Low's treatment and untiring care, the severe physical symptoms became less urgent, and in due time Sullivan's mind cleared.

The following account is taken from the written statement of his experience in Konnor Old House:

"On reaching the house he entered as noiselessly as possible, and made for the library, finding his way by the help of a series of matches to Sir James's couch, upon which he lay down. He was conscious at once of an acrid taste in his mouth, which he accounted for by the clouds of dust he had raised in crossing the room.

"First he began to think about the approaching football match with Scotland, for which he was already in training. He was still in his mood of derisive incredulity. The house seemed vastly empty, and wrapped in an uneasy silence, a silence which made each of his comfortable movements an omen of significance. Presently the sense of a presence in the room was borne in upon him. He sat up, and spoke softly. He almost expected someone to answer him, and so strong did this feeling become that he called out: 'Who's there?' No reply came, and he sat on amidst the oppressive silence. He says the slightest noise would have been a relief. It was the listening in the silence that bred in him so intense a longing to grapple with some solid opponent.

"Fear! He, who had denied the very existence of cause for fear, found himself shivering with an untranslatable terror! This was fear! He realised it with an infinite recoil of anger.

"Presently he became aware that the darkness about him was clearing. A feeble light filtered slowly through it from above. Looking up at the ceiling, he perceived directly above his head an irregular patch of pale phosphorescent luminance, which grew gradually brighter. How long he sat with his head thrown back, staring at the light, he does not know. It seemed years. Then he spoke to himself plainly. With an immense effort, he forced his eyes away from the light and got upon his feet to drag his limbs round the room. The phosphorescence was of a greenish tint, and as strong as moonlight, but the dust rose like vapour at the slightest movement, and somewhat obscured its power. He moved about, but not for long. A clogging weight, such as one feels in nightmare, pressed upon him, and his exhaustion was intensified by the overpowering physical disgust bred in him by the repulsive odour which passed across his face as he staggered back to the couch.

"For a few moments he would not look up. He says he had an impression that someone was watching him through the radiance as through a window. The atmosphere about him was thickening and cloaking the walls with drowsy horror, while his senses revolted and choked at the growing odour. Then followed a state of semi-sleep, for he recollects no more until he found himself staring again at the luminous patch on the ceiling.

"By this time the brightness was beginning to dim; dark smears showed through it here and there, which ran slowly together till out of them grew and protruded a fat, black, evil face. A second later Sullivan was aware that the horrible face was sinking down nearer and nearer to his own, while all about it the light changed to black, dripping fluid, that formed great drops and fell.

"It seemed as if he could not save himself; he could not move! The fighting blood in him had died out; Then fear, mad fear and strong loathing gave him the strength to act. He saw his own hand working savagely, it passed through and through the impending face, yet he swears that he felt a slight impact and that he saw the fat, glazed skin quiver! Then, with a final struggle, he tore it himself from the couch, and, rushing to the door, he wrenched open, and plunged forward into a red vacancy, down--down--After that he remembered no more."

While Sullivan still lay ill and unable to give an account of himself or of what had happened at Konnor Old House, Mr. Flaxman Low expressed his intention of paying a visit to the asylum for the purpose of seeing young Bowie. But on arrival at the asylum, he found that Bowie had died during the previous night. A weary-eyed assistant doctor took Mr. Low to see the body. Bowie had evidently been of a gaunt, but powerful build. The features, though harsh, were noble, the face being somewhat disfigured by a rough, raised discoloration, which extended from the centre of the forehead to behind the right ear.

Mr. Low asked a question.

"Yes, it is a very obscure case," observed the assistant, "but it is the disease he died of. When he was brought here some months ago he had a small dark spot on his forehead, but it spread rapidly, and there are now similar large patches over the whole of his body. I take it to be of a cancerous character, likely to occur in a scrofulous subject after a shock and severe mental strain, such as Bowie chose to subject himself to by passing a night in Konnor Old House. The first result of the shock was the imbecility, an increasing lethargic condition of the body supervened and finally coma."

While the doctor was speaking, Mr. Low bent over the dead man and closely examined the mark upon the face.

"This mark appears to be the result of a fungoid growth, perhaps akin to the Indian disease known as mycetoma?" he said at length.

"It may be so. The case is very obscure, but the disease, whatever we may call it, appears to be in Bowie's family, for I believe his uncle, Sir James Mackian, had precisely similar symptoms during his last illness. He also died in this institution, but that was before my time," replied the assistant.

After a further examination of the body Mr. Low took his leave, and during the following day or two was busily engaged in a spare empty room placed at his disposal by Naripse. A deal table and chair were all he required, Mr. Low explained, and to these he added a microscope, an apparatus for producing a moist heat, and the coat worn by Sullivan on the night of his adventure. At the end of the third day, as Sullivan was already on the road to recovery, Mr. Low, accompanied by Naripse, paid a second visit to Konnor Old House, during which Low mentioned some of his conclusions about the strange events which had occurred there. It will be an easy task to compare Mr. Flaxman Low's theory with the experience detailed by Sullivan and with the one or two subsequent discoveries that added something like confirmation to his conclusions.

Mr. Low and his host drove up as on the previous occasion, and stabled the horse as before. The day was dry, but grey, and the time the early afternoon. As they ascended the path leading to the house, Mr. Low remarked, after gazing up for a few seconds at the library window:

"That room has the air of being occupied."

"Why?--What makes you think so?" asked Naripse nervously.

"It is hard to say, but it produces that impression." Naripse shook his head despondently.

"I've always noticed it myself," he returned, "I wish Sullivan were all right again and able to tell us what he saw in there. Whatever it was it has nearly cost him his life. I don't suppose we shall ever know anything more definite about the matter."

"I fancy I can tell you," replied Low, "but let us get on into the library, and see what it looks like before we enter into the subject any further. By the way, I should advise you to tie your handkerchief over your mouth and nose before we go into the room."

Naripse, upon whom the events of the last few days had had a very strong effect, was in a state of scarcely-controllable excitement.

"What do you mean, Low?--you can't have any idea---"

"Yes, I believe the dust in that house to be simply poisonous. Sullivan inhaled any amount of it--hence his condition."

The same suggestion of loneliness and stagnation hung about the house as they passed through the hall and entered the library. They halted at the door and looked in. The amount of greenish dust in the room was extraordinary; it lay in little drifts and mounds over the floor, but most abundantly just about the couch. Immediately above this spot, they perceived on the ceiling a long, discoloured stain. Naripse pointed to it.

"Do you see that? It is a bloodstain, and, I give you my word, it grows larger and larger every year!" He finished the sentence in a low voice, and shuddered.

"Ah, so I should have expected," observed Flaxman Low, who was looking at the stained ceiling with much interest. "That, of course, explains everything."

"Low, tell me what you mean? A bloodstain that grows year by year explains everything?" Naripse broke off and pointed to the couch. "Look there! a cat's been walking over that sofa."

Mr. Low put his hand on his friend's shoulder and smiled.

"My dear fellow! That stain on the ceiling is simply a patch of mould and fungi, Now come in carefully without raising the dust, and let us examine the cat's footsteps, as you call them."

Naripse advanced to the couch and considered the marks gravely.

"They are not the footmarks of any animal, they are something much more unaccountable. They are raindrops. And why should raindrops be here in this perfectly watertight room, and even then only in one small part of it? You can't very well explain that, and you certainly can't have expected it?"

"Look round and follow my points," replied Mr. Low. "When we came to fetch Sullivan, I noticed the dust which far exceeds the ordinary accumulation even in the most neglected places. You may also notice that it is of a greenish colour and of extreme fineness. This dust is of the same nature as the powder you find in a puff-ball, and is composed of minute sporuloid bodies. I found that Sullivan's coat was covered with this fine dust, and also about the collar and upper portion of the sleeve I found one or two gummy drops which correspond to these raindrops, as you call them. I naturally concluded from their position that they had fallen from above. From the dust, or rather spores, which I found on Sullivan's coat, I have since cultivated no fewer than four specimens of fungi, of which three belong to known African species; but the fourth, so far as I know, has never been described, but it approximates most closely to one of the phalliodei."

"But how about the raindrops, or whatever they are? I believe they drop from that horrible stain."

"They are drops from the stain, and are caused by the unnamed fungus I have just alluded to. It matures very rapidly, and absolutely decays as it matures, liquefying into a sort of dark mucilage, full of spores, which drips down, and diffuses a most repulsive odour. In time the mucilage dries, leaving the dust of the spores."

"I don't know much about these things myself," replied Naripse dubiously, "and it strikes me you know more than enough. But look here; how about the light? You saw it last night yourself."

"It happens that the three species of African fungi possess well known phosphorescent properties, which are manifested not only during decomposition, but also during the period of growth. The light is only visible from time to time; probably climatic and atmospheric conditions only admit of occasional efflorescence."

"But," object Naripse, "supposing it to be a case of poisoning by fungi as you say, how is it that Sullivan, though exposed to precisely the same sources of danger as the others who have passed a night here, has escaped? He has been very ill, but his mind has already regained its balance, whereas, in the three other cases, the mind was wholly destroyed."

Mr. Low looked very grave.

"My dear fellow, you are such an excitable and superstitious person that I hesitate to put your nerves to any further test."

"Oh, go on!"

"I hesitate for two reasons. The one I have mentioned, and also because in my answer I must speak of curious and unpleasant things, some of which are proved facts, others only more or less well-founded assumptions. It is acknowledged that fungi exert an important influence in certain diseases, a few being directly attributable to fungi as a primary cause. Also it is an historical fact that poisonous fungi have more than once been used to alter the fate of nations. From the evidence before us and the condition of Bowie's body, I can but conclude that the unknown fungus I have alluded to is of a singularly malignant nature, and acts through the skin upon the brain with terrible rapidity afterwards gradually inter-penetrating all the tissues of the body, and eventually causing death. In Sullivan's case, luckily, the falling drops only touched his clothing, not his skin."

"But wait a minute, Low, how did these fungi come here? And how can we rid the house of them? Upon my word, it is enough to make a man go off his head to hear about it. What are you going to do now?"

"In the first place we will go upstairs and examine the flooring just above that stained patch of ceiling."

"You can't do that I'm afraid. The room above this happens to be divided into two portions by a hollow partition between 2ft. and 3ft. thick," said Naripse, "the interior of which may originally have been meant for a cupboard, but I don't think it has ever been used."

"Then let us examine the cupboard; there must be some way of getting into it."

Upon this Naripse led the way upstairs, but, as he gained the top, he leant back, and grasping Mr. Low by the arm thrust him violently forward.

"Look! the light--did you see the light?" he said.

For a second or two it seemed as if a light, like the elusive light thrown by a rotating reflector, quivered on the four walls of the landing, then disappeared almost before one could he certain of having seen it.

"Can you point me out the precise spot where you saw the shining figure you told us of?" asked Low.

Naripse pointed to a dark corner of the landing.

"Just there in front of that panel between the two doors. Now that I come to think of it, I fancy there is some means of opening the upper part of that panel. The idea was to ventilate the cupboard-like space I mentioned just now."

Naripse walked across the landing and felt round the panel, till he found a small metal knob. On turning this, the upper part of the panel fell back like a shutter, disclosing a narrow space of darkness beyond. Naripse thrust his head into the opening and peered into the gloom, but immediately started back with a gasp.

"The shining man!" he cried. "He's there!"

Mr. Flaxman Low, hardly knowing what to expect, looked over his shoulder; then, exerting his strength, pulled away some of the lower boarding. For within, at arm's length, stood a dimly shining figure! A tall man, with his back towards them, leaning against the left of the partition, and shrouded from head to foot in faintly luminous white mould.

The figure remained quite motionless while they stared at it in surprise; then Mr. Flaxman Low pulled on his glove, and, leaning forward, touched the man's head. A portion of the white mass came away in his fingers, the lower surface of which showed a bunch of frizzled negroid hair.

"Good Heavens, Low, what do you make of this?" asked Naripse. "It must be the body of Jake. But what is this shining stuff?"

Low stood under the wide skylight and examined what he held in his fingers.

"Fungus," he said at last. "And it appears to have some property allied to the mouldy fungus which attacks the common house-fly. Have you not seen them dead upon window-panes, stiffly fixed upon their legs, and covered with a white mould? Something of the same kind has taken place here."

"But what had Jake to do with the fungus? And how did he come here?"

"All that, of course, we can only surmise," replied Mr. Low. "There is little doubt that secrets of nature hidden from us are well known to the various African tribes. It is possible that the negro possessed some of these deadly spores, but how or why he made use of them are questions that can never be cleared up now."

"But what was he doing here?" asked Naripse.

"As I said before we can only guess the answer to that question, but I should suppose that the negro made use of this cupboard as a place where he could be free from interruption; that he here cultivated the spores is proved by the condition of his body and of the ceiling immediately below. Such an occupation is by no means free from danger, especially in an airless and inclosed space such as this. It is evident that either by design or accident he became infected by the fungus poison, which in time covered his whole body as you now see. The subject of obeah," Flaxman Low went on reflectively, "is one to the study of which I intend to devote myself at some future period. I have, indeed, already made some arrangements for an expedition in connection with the subject into the interior of Africa."

"And how is the horrible thing to be got rid of? Nothing short of burning the place down would be of any radical use," remarked Naripse.

Low, who by this time was deeply engrossed in considering the strange facts with which he had just become acquainted, answered abstractedly: "I suppose not."

Naripse said no more, and the words were only recalled to Mr. Low's mind a day or two later, when he received by post a copy of the West Coast Advertiser. It was addressed in the handwriting of Naripse, and the following extract was lightly scored:

"Konnor Old House, the property of Thomas Naripse, Esquire, of Konnor Lodge, was, we regret to say, destroyed by fire last night. We are sorry to add that the loss to the owner will be considerable, as no insurance policy had been effected with regard to the property."

Collected Ghost Stories - 22 stories
M. R. James
Benediction Classics, 2011
284 pages
ISBN: 978-1-84902-454-9
Available from www.amazon.com,
www.amazon.co.uk

Collected Ghost Stories by M R James is a collection of twenty-two ghost stories, plus a fascinating essay on the writing of ghost stories. The collection is comprised of the following twenty-two stories: The Uncommon Prayer-Book; A Neighbour's Landmark; Rats; The Experiment; The Malice Of Inanimate Objects; A Vignette; Canon Alberic's Scrap-Book; The Stalls Of Barchester Cathedral; An Episode Of Cathedral History; The Story Of A Disappearance And An Appearance; The Haunted Dolls' House; Lost Hearts; Mr. Humphreys And His Inheritance; Martin's Close; The Diary Of Mr. Poynter; The Rose-Garden; Casting The Runes; A School Story; The Tractate Middoth; Two Doctors; A View From A Hill; The Residence At Whitminster; Appendix: M. R. James On Ghost Stories Note: This is not to be confused with the Book "The Collected Ghost Stories of M R James" which was published in 1931.

The Weird Menace Collection
Robert Ervin Howard
Benediction Classics, 2011
182 pages
ISBN: 978-1-84902-450-1
Available from www.amazon.com,
www.amazon.co.uk

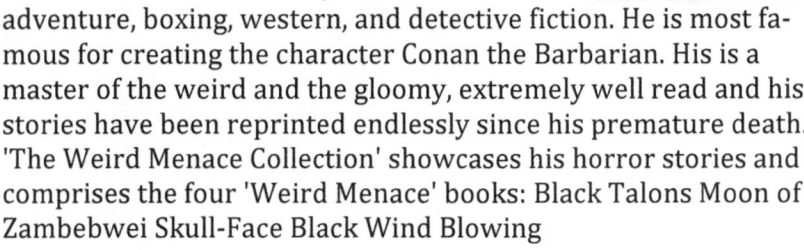

Robert Ervin Howard (1906 - 1936) was an American writer of fantasy, horror, historical adventure, boxing, western, and detective fiction. He is most famous for creating the character Conan the Barbarian. His is a master of the weird and the gloomy, extremely well read and his stories have been reprinted endlessly since his premature death. 'The Weird Menace Collection' showcases his horror stories and comprises the four 'Weird Menace' books: Black Talons Moon of Zambebwei Skull-Face Black Wind Blowing

Collected Twilight Stories - 18 Twilight tales
Marjorie Bowen

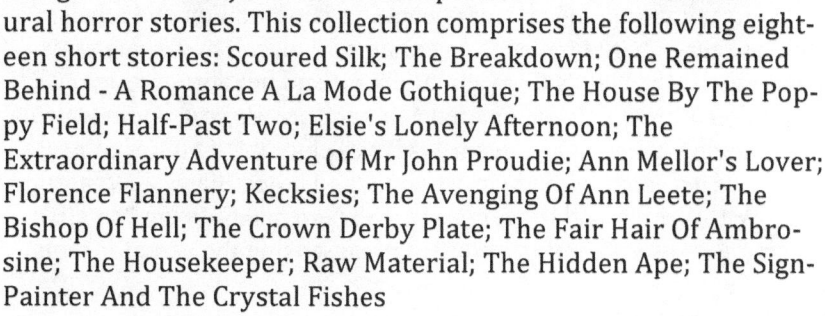

Oxford City Press, 2011
266 pages
ISBN: 978-1-84902-453-2

Available from www.amazon.com, www.amazon.co.uk

Collected Twilight Stories' is a compilation of eighteen of Marjorie Bowen's supernatural horror stories. This collection comprises the following eighteen short stories: Scoured Silk; The Breakdown; One Remained Behind - A Romance A La Mode Gothique; The House By The Poppy Field; Half-Past Two; Elsie's Lonely Afternoon; The Extraordinary Adventure Of Mr John Proudie; Ann Mellor's Lover; Florence Flannery; Kecksies; The Avenging Of Ann Leete; The Bishop Of Hell; The Crown Derby Plate; The Fair Hair Of Ambrosine; The Housekeeper; Raw Material; The Hidden Ape; The Sign-Painter And The Crystal Fishes

The Power of Darkness and other Chilling Tales
Edith Nesbit

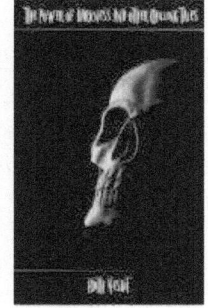

Benediction Classics, 2012
68 pages
ISBN: 978-1-78139-190-7

Available from www.amazon.com, www.amazon.co.uk

Edith Nesbit is best known as the author of The Railway Children, but she was also a great writer of terror and ghost stories. Do not read this book at bedtime or you may be haunted in the night! Nesbit spins chilling tales, where we meet the undead, love transcends the grave, vampires stalk us and ghosts have their vengeance. These spooky stories, tinged with horror, are vibrant and bold, spanning the years to come and scare us today. In this collection are: Power of Darkness; Man-Size in Marble; John Charrington's Wedding; In the Dark; The Mystery of the Semi-Detached; The Ebony Frame.

Also from Benediction Books …
Wandering Between Two Worlds: Essays on Faith and Art
Anita Mathias
Benediction Books, 2007
152 pages
ISBN: 0955373700

Available from www.amazon.com, www.amazon.co.uk

In these wide-ranging lyrical essays, Anita Mathias writes, in lush, lovely prose, of her naughty Catholic childhood in Jamshedpur, India; her large, eccentric family in Mangalore, a sea-coast town converted by the Portuguese in the sixteenth century; her rebellion and atheism as a teenager in her Himalayan boarding school, run by German missionary nuns, St. Mary's Convent, Nainital; and her abrupt religious conversion after which she entered Mother Teresa's convent in Calcutta as a novice. Later rich, elegant essays explore the dualities of her life as a writer, mother, and Christian in the United States-- Domesticity and Art, Writing and Prayer, and the experience of being "an alien and stranger" as an immigrant in America, sensing the need for roots.

About the Author

Anita Mathias is the author of *Wandering Between Two Worlds: Essays on Faith and Art.* She has a B.A. and M.A. in English from Somerville College, Oxford University, and an M.A. in Creative Writing from the Ohio State University, USA. Anita won a National Endowment of the Arts fellowship in Creative Nonfiction in 1997. She lives in Oxford, England with her husband, Roy, and her daughters, Zoe and Irene.

Anita's website:
   http://www.anitamathias.com, and
Anita's blog Dreaming Beneath the Spires:
   http://dreamingbeneaththespires.blogspot.com

The Church That Had Too Much
Anita Mathias
Benediction Books, 2010
52 pages
ISBN: 9781849026567

Available from www.amazon.com, www.amazon.co.uk

The Church That Had Too Much was very well-intentioned. She
wanted to love God, she wanted to love people, but she was both hampered by her muchness and the abundance of her possessions, and
beset by ambition, power struggles and snobbery. Read about the sur-
prising way The Church That Had Too Much began to resolve her
problems in this deceptively simple and enchanting fable.

About the Author

Anita Mathias is the author of *Wandering Between Two Worlds: Essays on Faith and Art*. She has a B.A. and M.A. in English from
Somerville College, Oxford University, and an M.A. in Creative Writing from the Ohio State University, USA. Anita won a National
Endowment of the Arts fellowship in Creative Nonfiction in 1997.
She lives in Oxford, England with her husband, Roy, and her daughters, Zoe and Irene.

Anita's website:
    http://www.anitamathias.com, and
Anita's blog Dreaming Beneath the Spires:
    http://dreamingbeneaththespires.blogspot.com

www.ingramcontent.com/pod-product-compliance
Lightning Source LLC
Chambersburg PA
CBHW020633130626
46552CB00003B/1213